THE WINGS OF MORNING

Other books by Douglas Atwill
from Boxwood Press

Douglas Atwill Houses
Bonfire
Yellow Eyes in the Garden
Fifty-Three Paintings
Seventy-One Poems
A Studio Year

THE WINGS OF MORNING

a novel

Douglas Atwill

BOXWOOD PRESS

Library of Congress Cataloging-in-Publication Data

Atwill, Douglas, author.
The Wings of Morning / by Douglas Atwill.
ISBN-13: 978-0-692-76011-6
Library of Congress Control Number: 2019908954

1. Writers 2. Artists 3. Southwest 4. Atwill, Douglas

Boxwood Press
PO Box 5959 Santa Fe NM 87502

Book design by
Kathleen Dexter/KD Ink and Image (*kdinkandimage.net*)

CONTENTS

If I take the wings of the morning,
and dwell in the uttermost parts of the sea;
Even there shall thy hand lead me,
and thy right hand shall hold me.

PSALMS 139

COD FILLETS WITH CAPER SAUCE

One July evening in the year 1946, the Summervilles and the Parchers were dining together on the terrace behind the Summerville mansion in a quiet enclave of Philadelphia. Before the war, Isabel Summerville was one of the city's accomplished hostesses and now that the strictures of food rationing had been loosened just a bit, she wanted to restart the gentle rhythm of her dinner parties with a simple family gathering, testing out the household staff before bringing over the more illustrious members of her large circle. In addition to this greater reason, Isaac Parcher had told her there were important family matters to discuss, to make a decision upon soon.

The Summerville house was famous for its fine stonework, with beveled Vermont granite arches over each of the windows, and for the superb elevated location looking out over the smaller houses in that part of the city. From the garden-front terrace the diners could see across the chestnut and elm trees of the nearby common ground from colonial times to the western horizon beyond, where the sun had gone behind a line of chrome-yellow clouds. Potted orange trees, brought by the gardeners out from the glass-walled orangerie for the summer, stood in a protecting crescent along the edge of the terrace, as if an uncivilized zone lay beyond

in the shadier reaches of the garden and real danger beyond
that. If the war had brought privations to most of Philadelphia, there was only a moderate lowering of the patterns of
privilege in this section on the town high-grounds.

Isabel Summerville decided to start her dinner early,
while the light was still good and the chill of evening had
yet to arrive. She knew that the sweet, mid-summer aroma from the blossoming London plane trees on the street
would course over the house and perfume the entire meal.
The candles down the middle of the table flickered, even
as they were protected from the slight breeze by columns
of etched glass. As she looked around at her family, Isabel
thought almost everybody looked better in the gentle light
of gloaming. The important family matters could wait until
after the main courses had already been consumed, when
good sense mingled with a full stomach.

There were eight at the dinner table, four Summervilles
and four Parchers, all easily at conversation while the covered plates of food arrived from the distant kitchen, extra
waiters hired to assist the usual staff. Isabel sat at the end
closest to the door with Isaac Parcher, the eldest of the gathered guests, to her right. Her husband, Borden Summerville, sat at the opposite end with Isaac's wife to his right.
Rank and position were honored in both of these families
whose forebears intertwined many times, with twice a pair
of brothers marrying a pair of sisters and several marriages
between second cousins to further complicate the matter. In
fact, in this generation Isabel Summerville and Augustine
Parcher were sisters from the Fairfax family. It was thought
but not often openly discussed that family fortunes could be
protected and enlarged this way, no unsymmetrical pairings
to allow leakage of the fortune onto the common pavement.

Isaac Parcher's family had always made money when the nation went to war, not from explosives, munitions or rifles, but by supplying the manifold necessary items such as helmets and helmet liners, brass buckles for military belts, water canteens, buttons for uniforms, spoons, forks, and the other ancillary objects made from metal that armies and navies required in great number. The Parcher fortune had started in the Civil War with Isaac's grandfather's brass-works, enlarged by his father before the Great War, with new factories and foundries purchased along the river. These fabricated anything out of metal and came into their finest bloom during World War II, when they were also able to supply canvas goods, leather goods, and even the particular papers that military men favored for their orders. The capital letter P in a circle identified the family in a stamp on the metal goods and an embroidered version on the articles made of cloth. A purchase from the Parcher factories contributed to every corner of the conflict, taken aboard freighters down the Delaware River and across the sea to the war depots across the globe.

At the other end of the table, Borden Summerville was an equally successful partner to the war efforts, his companies financing, underwriting, mortgaging, and insuring the participants of national battle. Summerville accounting firms kept track of the profits of the many other Philadelphia wartime businesses, keeping shadow ledgers if required. The capital letter S, also in a circle, identified a Summerville business, an idea no doubt agreed to at a similar intrafamily dinner many decades ago, when a roasted joint and Yorkshire pudding would have been more typical.

All the dinner guests would be horrified and embarrassed to hear the words that war was good for their families, but it was true. Now that peace had arrived, with their coffers overflowing, it was a time for contemplation and reassessment. The talk among the men was of new businesses, ventures in the western states and perhaps overseas. Few of the eight people had actually travelled in the recent past to the west or abroad, but it was a subject brought up almost every day now. A new age was hearing the first notes of the overture, and all was possible. The families would partake of their share.

Isaac's wife, Augustine, sat on Borden Summerville's right, as was proper. The eldest woman should be on the host's right. At these family gatherings, it was often Augustine who started new tracks of conversation or cut off any disagreeable topic, a role often taken up by the men in other families. Her blue eyes missed very little going on at her sister's table and her dark hair had no sign of gray intrusions. She had been listening to Borden's finely detailed account of the Summerville Bank's new actuarial department, he deciding to catch up his sister-in-law on a full war's worth of news. Like Livia in ancient Rome, she decided to kill this child before it thrived any further.

"Borden, dear," Augustine said, "let's move along. What news of your younger sister?"

"I was going to bring the subject of Malvina up later, but now is just as good. She is well, to start with, but getting on in her years."

"Alas. What of her school, out in the wilds of New Mexico?"

"It's not in the wilds, Augustine, but in the capital city of Santa Fe."

"Nonetheless. When is she finally coming back again to Philadelphia, where she was born?"

"Never, I expect." Borden paused, as he was the last at the table to ladle out a serving of asparagus cream soup from the tureen held by a servant. "She left thirty some years ago and still loves living out west."

"And she never married after that fiasco at the church altar?"

"No, but she has a life-long companion. An artist she befriended."

"How long now has this been going on?"

"Thirty some years now."

"Curious. Malvina herself built most of the school, did she not?"

"Yes. Sometimes laying up the adobes and doing much of the carpentry and woodwork. Difficult work for a woman, but she wrote me that she loved it. Twenty separate buildings over six or seven years. I've saved her letters from back then. She seemed so happy. The school took a while to establish itself, but by the thirties it was well attended. Young teachers came from Boston and San Francisco. Local teachers taught Spanish and French. There was even a Chinese Geometry teacher, a distant cousin of Madame Chiang Kai-Shek. Girls from many good families attended Summerville School, even from the East Coast."

"I don't know any," Augustine said, thinking how annoying it was that her brother-in-law Borden tended to over-describe most matters, losing the clear track for the details. How was such a scatterbrain able to run a bank so successfully?

Borden continued, "Her artist friend, Alberta Todd, meanwhile, gained quite a reputation. They went together to New York for her exhibits. Her fame added to the luster of the school."

"I have heard of her, Borden."

The soup plates were cleared and the fish course arrived, a small gold-circled plate of filleted cod with a green caper sauce. Augustine was not convinced that good things could actually happen in the west. The center of her world and all suitable worlds was here in the city of brotherly love, where the massive horse-chestnuts lined each side of the granite paved streets and family lineages back through half-a-dozen layers were known by all. In her mind, roads to the provinces left in all directions like Rome, but the center was the center, after all.

"I recall Malvina as a girl," Augustine said, "both of us in the same level at Pinetree Academy for Girls. She was a tomboy, a hero to the girls' hockey team. Not so very good at the books, however."

"She had her own sort of poetry, we thought," Borden said, trying to stay loyal to his absent sister. "I went to Santa Fe for a visit before the war on my way to a business meeting on the West Coast. By then her school had a great charm about it, handsome adobe buildings on a terraced hill above the eastern part of the city. She remembered her family home in the wooden trim she fashioned around the doors and windows, federal-style pediments and Greek Key borders. Beautiful, many-paned windows and classic proportions everywhere the eye landed. She planted apple and pear trees early on and they were all in bloom. Boxwood borders. The young students performed a modern dance for us, a paean to the Goddess Pomona in a garden with stone Ionic columns."

"I can't think it was equivalent to our beloved Pinetree Academy. The Goddess Pomona, indeed."

"You are right, of course, Augustine, but there was a certain style and elegance there. No log cabin rawness as you imply. I was proud to be Malvina's brother."

At the other end of the table Isabel and Isaac were also talking about Santa Fe and the errant Summerville sister so far away from the filleted cod they were finishing, lightly spooning up the last swirls of the caper sauce. Isabel looked around the table with the sharp eye of an able hostess, checking how the fish course was being received and to what level the wine glasses had fallen.

"Malvina is Borden's favorite sister," she said to Isaac, "and he will hear nothing bad about her. I hope Augustine is not treading too heavily down there. I, also, adore Malvina, but there is news."

"She wants to sell the school, I understand."

"Lock, stock, and barrel. You already know. Borden is so concerned about what she will do thereafter. She talks of Europe or a world tour. Writing her memoirs."

"I believe that her trust is still held here in Philadelphia."

"Of course."

"I have a proposition for you to present to Borden, after dinner, of course. Just to keep it in the family, I will buy the Summerville School for Owen. He's been a restless son here in Philadelphia after the war and keeps trying out his painting skills. His studio on Elm Street is too small and dark, and he yearns for something he does not quite know. They say the light in New Mexico is extraordinary, not unlike Provence. The twenty buildings at the school should be enough for his endeavors, and I can't think it would not be a good investment in the end for the other family trusts."

"Splendid idea and it might not be a very bad thing to have your son away from the city while he's sowing his oats. Unsavory things can happen to artists. Haven't you made a place for him at the factories?"

"The war changed him. He came back with no interest in brass fittings or canvas tents. It was a sad day for me."

"You are a good man, Isaac."

"I know that Owen is talented and needs to try this painting thing out. I want to give him his chance. He is twenty-four now, still young enough for this artistic trial. In time, I trust he will return to his senses. Perhaps Santa Fe will rush things along. Let us hope, Isabel."

"I will speak to Borden about the purchase when all of you have gone home. You remember that he is still the lead trustee of Malvina's trust."

"I do. It seems a sensible solution to several problems, never going outside the family."

Isaac's neighbor at the table, a younger Parcher, leaned over and asked whom they were talking so seriously about.

"Malvina. She wants to sell her school out west."

"Oh rats, I've always wanted to visit her there."

"Well, you can visit Owen instead."

The meal progressed through other courses – meats, salads, desserts, cheeses and savories — as the conversation turned to other matters, and the coffee was served in German blue-and-white porcelain cups inside the sitting room as the gloaming light on the terrace turned to dark. Afterwards the family scattered to nearby parts of Philadelphia as Isabel and Borden walked upstairs and to bed. The selling and purchase of Malvina's Summerville School as a gift for Owen Parcher was agreed to as they were settling down, Borden's abundant white hair safely away from mussing in a specially knit, pull-on cotton cap. Isabel felt rewarded in her role as the discreet go-between, ensuring that a property title would glissando from Malvina to her nephew Owen, requiring a substantial sum of money with no prying outside eyes as witness. She also knew that the engines of her entertaining skills were coming alive again, unused, unoiled, and quiet for so long.

The actual selling price was never discussed, since it was a transfer of ownership from the Summerville side to the Parcher side. For as long as anybody remembered, they were considered to be but one family. Isabel was the last to switch off the light and turn onto her side, back-to-back with Borden who was already wheezing his way to sleep.

THE ELM STREET STUDIO

It was a four-story, fieldstone building, built on Philadelphia's Lower Elm Street in the middle of the last century to house a family of middle-class Bavarian immigrants, using the ground floor as the hardware store and the upper ones for living quarters. Over the years that part of Philadelphia had become of lesser value and the house, after a succession of changes, was now owned by an old brother and sister who ran a small grocery on the street floor – an assortment of canned goods, dry goods, bottled beverages kept cold, a cursory selection of wilted produce, and large faceted glass jars of vinegar with full-sized, dill pickles and peeled hard-boiled eggs at the cash register – leaving the three floors above completely vacant. The brother and sister lived elsewhere nearby, so it was a good news day when Theodore Parcher asked to lease their three upper floors as a studio for his nephew, Owen. He paid them a year's rent in advance and said his nephew would be responsible for it thereafter, when he returned from his army service overseas. He painted a rosy picture of Owen's steadfastness, bravery, and talent.

The war came to an end, and after a day or two at home in the big house on the hill, Owen moved over to the Elm Street rooms. The Parcher household staff helped him on

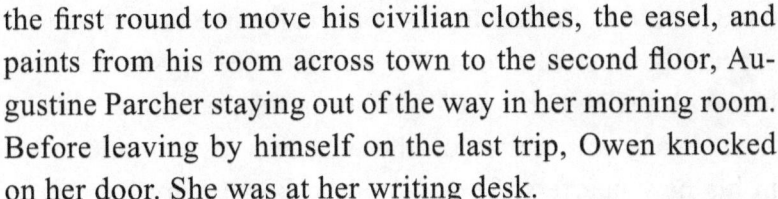

the first round to move his civilian clothes, the easel, and paints from his room across town to the second floor, Augustine Parcher staying out of the way in her morning room. Before leaving by himself on the last trip, Owen knocked on her door. She was at her writing desk.

"Sit down, Owen," she said. "You know I am upset about this. It was wrong for Theodore to arrange this separate studio business behind our backs."

"No, it was good he did it, and I will be only a few miles away," Owen said.

"It will seem like more. A serpent's tooth, indeed."

"I need a place of my own, Mother. There are issues about the war that I need to sort out. You are always welcome to visit."

"Lucky me, making an appointment with my own son."

"Without an appointment. Anytime."

"Your father is somehow complicit in this. He was always too lenient."

"No, blame his brother Theodore if you must. Papa just wants everybody to be happy."

"*I'm* not happy. But, I shall make myself get accustomed to it. And I shall confront Theodore in my own time about this."

"I love you, Mother."

"You may now call me Augustine, to mirror our new more distant relationship."

She waved her hand for him to get out. It was a relief for him for this exchange to be over. He had read somewhere about the necessity of prying the keys away from the father, becoming a man, but in this family it was clearly the mother who kept the hidden keys of power under her pillow. Owen was not sure he actually now had the symbolic keys in his hand, as it did not feel that he was really free or that he was especially more of a man. Maybe those feelings would follow with the keys ringing together in his pocket.

A heavy rain pelted on the windows as he made order in his new quarters. Sims would be home from Europe in three weeks and he would take the third floor as his writing studio. They would share the living space on the top floor where there was both a kitchen and a bathroom. He missed Sims, who was always a calming influence on those around him. There were heavy seas back home for Sims to calm.

By early afternoon he was ready to start on the first canvas, a forty-inch square. The painting table had the fat, full tubes of oil paint in military rows, an unused rainbow.

He knew it would not go well at first, but remembered the advice from an old painting professor at Princeton: *Get quickly into the middle of things.* Within a few hours the canvas had the "first covering" as they said back at school, color over all the surface but not necessarily in the correct places. He could now take his time refining, scraping away, or adding new ideas. It was a good first day.

The following weeks, before Sims arrived, he worked assiduously on half-a-dozen canvases without hearing a word from the stone house on the other side of town. He knew he would eventually give in and start meeting his parents for dinner or lunch, start repairing the hurt this studio had caused. But right now, he felt the wings of a new morning taking him up, and up, freeing him from the earthly matters far below, as he looked at the canvases leaning against the walls. They were not perfect, he was sure, but he could see the way forward, to where something closer to perfection might lie.

Just then, the doorbell at the bottom of the stairs rang. It was his mother in her battle gear, a wide-brimmed hat and a fox stole, stopping by before what would amount to an afternoon of luncheon combat in Philadelphia society. Owen could not help but think it might have been better for her to go to war in Europe than himself. Were the true warriors in his family the women? He thought of a flotilla of triremes filled with Parcher and Summerville women, round shields on the railings like breasts, spears erect, terrifying the men ashore as they approached.

"Odd smell in here, Owen."

"Turpentine and linseed oil."

"Not just that. I'll open a window."

"I have some coffee here. Would you like a cup?"

Owen was a neat and tidy man, even before the army years, his room in order every morning. He had placed a table and chairs across the studio, where he could sit and study what was going on at the easel and the displayed canvases against the far wall. He motioned for his mother to sit down. They drank their coffee and talked a while about his paintings, what he had in mind, how well it was coming out.

"But, I don't think," Owen said, "that art appreciation is the reason for your visit."

"No, indeed. I've been thinking, Owen."

"I suspected so."

"Now hear me out and don't interrupt. The subject is men like you coming back from the war. Often with mental wounds they cannot describe. Shellshock we called it after the First War, the hurt of not being able to erase the sound of bombs and images of bloodied comrades dead on the ground or dying. My uncles both had it and neither was ever quite the same afterwards, even with their admirable wives. The farms suffered."

"May I say? I do not have shellshock. Sims has written that he has been hearing the rocket bombs in his sleep, but I'm okay."

"I know that, son, but something has turned you away from your family. Made you look off in a different direction than the son I remember."

"That is true. It well could have happened without the war."

"I don't think so. Unlike many young men we know, you did not see actual combat, but were in London in an office. That does not comport with blood and bombs."

"That is also true. But being so near to war makes a change, too. Seeing friends go away and not return. Hearing explosions on the next block and surviving."

"I believe you are taking the war as an excuse to shirk your family duty of work with your father, becoming a proper heir to what he has grown. What we both have expected."

"That could be. Men grow up and want a different way from their parents. It has happened throughout time, in times of peace as well. Man grows up, leaves home."

"I also have the strong view that getting back into the fold of the family is the best cure for your malaise. Working with your father and cousins every day, keeping a schedule has a soothing quality, healing whatever it is."

"I am doing just that sort of healing here."

"So you are determined to ignore me?"

"I think so, Mother."

"Your father is grievously sad, Owen."

"I'm sorry. I don't believe I can help it. I'm different."

"I don't how you came to be so different."

"I always was. You just couldn't see."

"Owen, I thought I ought to try."

"I know, Mother. Thank you."

"I don't want to believe that you are just being selfish and willful."

"I'm glad, because I'm not."

"Very well. Come to lunch tomorrow. Just at twelve."

Mother and son hugged, and she made quickly for the stairs. Owen knew that what he did not say, that he was homosexual and loved his cousin Sims, would have to be said at some later time. He had met other men in London like himself and knew that many American men coming home were going through the same dilemma, the war bringing about their first truthful discussions.

It was a matter that he must first talk about with his father, Isaac, who might possibly understand. Somewhere in the back of his mind there was the thought that Isaac might be homosexual, too, but he had been not strong enough to fight the pressures from his own parents to marry, to go the other way. He and Sims one night in London made a list of the many men in Philadelphia who might be the same, as well as the unmarried members from several generations back in their conjoined families. They found dozens of suspected homosexuals hiding in plain sight, including both their fathers. Sims had read more on the matter than Owen and claimed that men had loved men from the beginning of time. Even before the Greeks, it was the natural way, he said. Owen was trying to catch up.

WIDE-BRIMMED SUN HATS

Malvina Summerville loved building and living at her school property in Santa Fe, a hillside now crowded with houses of varying sizes, some quite grand with entrance verandas and double entry doors and others more spare, mere mud-walled cottages of a few rooms with low ceilings of peeled logs. The two existing century-old houses had been encircled in the newly built buildings that looked as old and venerable as the others. Walkways and steps ran from house to house, giving the sense of a small, perched village in the south of France or an Italian hill town, high walls guarding against foreign invaders from the valley. With a sense of pride, Malvina felt that the school was a smaller version of Santa Fe itself, the grand next to the low all together on winding streets and lanes, like an egalitarian stew of fine meats, reduced wines, and simple rice, carrots, and potatoes. Now it had been sold to her nephew, newly a civilian after discharge from the US Army.

It had been thirty some years since Malvina laid the first footings on the new buildings, and the Summerville School appeared as if it had been there since the beginning of time. Vines grew on many of the walls, and apple trees were now past maturity, the gnarled branches evidence of repeated prunings and harvests. The stone and adobe wall circled the

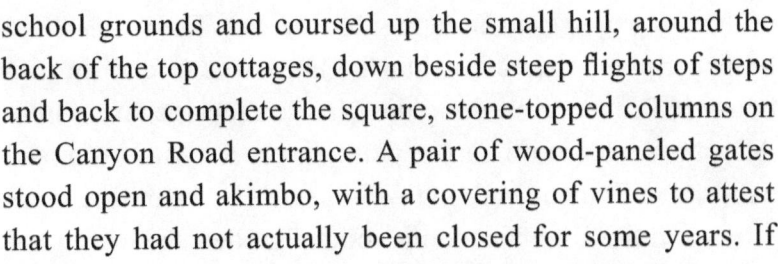

school grounds and coursed up the small hill, around the back of the top cottages, down beside steep flights of steps and back to complete the square, stone-topped columns on the Canyon Road entrance. A pair of wood-paneled gates stood open and akimbo, with a covering of vines to attest that they had not actually been closed for some years. If buildings can exude a sense of well-being, these did.

The property looked larger than the four acres it included, probably because of the many houses so very close together, and there were still open areas not built upon. The flat area of grass on the lower level showed little evidence of its past as a hockey field, even the goal posts were nowhere to be seen now. A few young trees had sprouted up along the edges of the field, seedlings from the massive cottonwoods adjoining the gates. But the grass center was clipped and trimmed.

Malvina had been attendant to maintaining such a large property over the years, especially difficult during the war when help was hard to find. It would be safe to say that the property was "burnished" but not in disrepair. Many a local family with masons and carpenters survived the lean Depression years on the Summerville paychecks. Their women worked in the school laundry and kitchen, and some taught Spanish and French to the young girls. The school was a beloved cottage industry to quite a few Santa Fe citizens and there was worry among them about what the future held.

Malvina and her companion, Alberta, were having their last Santa Fe breakfast on the portal of the large house to the side of the front lawn. The help would come in later to take away the dishes. Train tickets to New York had been purchased, where they would board the newly refurbished Queen Mary for a September crossing to Southampton, one of the first voyages to Europe since the war. The women had no exact plans thereafter, but the hope was to end up in a house in Provence or along the Mediterranean coast, where Alberta would continue her painting career with promised exhibits in France. Malvina would start her memoirs, plant citrus and the abundant semi-tropical garden she had in her mind, with an annotated horticultural guide tucked away in her luggage. They would, she felt sure, find a suitable English touring car with a cloth top in London, cross the Channel and motor slowly to the south, Malvina priding herself on her capable driving. They had purchased leather driving gloves and a selection of wide-brimmed sun hats for the journey, open air much preferable to closed windows and a stuffy interior. Rainy days would surely not be a bother.

The two women would be noticed on their journey, Alberta's lofty, patrician bearing a perfect foil to Malvina's more sturdy stance, the tall always finding the short, the willowy branch finding the oaken trunk. Malvina had a selection of tweed trousers made up for the trip, sensible outfits for travel. Perhaps there would be a property to buy, but surely they would find a handsome house to lease while they looked. Their three decades in Santa Fe were over, new adventures waiting in the recovering Europe for these two women.

"I don't remember much about Owen...Wennie, as we called him," Malvina said as she buttered her toast, "but the fact that he wants to paint and not be an industrialist like Isaac is greatly to his credit. I recall him on that trip I took back to Philadelphia in the Twenties, a solemn six-year-old at the dinner table. No doubt some unsavory stories had preceded me. He kept staring at me as if I were a giraffe, holding his spoon motionless over the soup bowl. Wide open, blue eyes. I wished then that I could make red smoke come out of the top of my head, just to make his eyes open wider. You remember him when they came here."

"I do. He's a handsome fellow now, from the photo you received," Alberta replied. "Good for him for remembering his aunt and wanting a different life like hers. I'm sorry we're not going to meet him next week, an awarded veteran, but so young."

"The war has made its mark on him, I am sure."

"Since he wants out of Philadelphia, it could be an improving mark instead of a bad one."

"I thought it better he arrive and see his Summerville School on his own. No family folderol to intercede on first impressions. He is a lucky young man, walking into a new life, fully funded by the Parcher factories and their smoking chimneys. His mother worries that he will marry a local girl and asked me to suggest an introduction to only the finer, old Spanish families."

"The ever-interfering sisters, Isabel and Augustine. I left your Owen a note and a small painting of the Cortland apples. On the writing table."

"A lovely touch."

"You will miss your Summerville School and all your belongings, Malvina. I can't think that they now all belong to Owen Parcher, thanks of course to Isaac."

"A clean sweep, but because of the very large payment to my portion, my trust fund is full to overflowing. There was a handsome increase in property value during our stay here. I suppose I'll miss the Packard Roadster, but little else."

"We had some lovely trips in her. The ruins at Chaco, to Mexico, to Santa Monica, and the weeks at Canyon de Chelly."

"I feel free, my feet not quite touching the ground."

"We'll see how long it lasts, won't we?"

The hired car arrived early with a quick honk to take them to the train station in Lamy, so the two women cut their breakfast short. An earlier van had already left with the luggage. They had expressly asked for the car to wait at the front gate, and the two women walked slowly across the lawn and turned around at the gate. A breeze pulled away a cascade of yellow leaves from the cottonwood tree, like a rain of confetti to mark the departure of a steamship.

"I wonder if we'll ever be back," Alberta asked as she closed her sun umbrella.

"Perhaps. They were happy years, weren't they?"

"Mostly, but not entirely."

RACK AND RUIN

L a Bajada hill was the steepest grade since the two men left the East Coast to drive west, angling this way and that up the switchbacks of the sharp escarpment. It flummoxed many earlier motorists coming west, thinking that the flat grasslands at the nation's center were all there was. The inadequate cooling systems of family sedans and trucks from the 1930s were not up to going uphill in a low gear for half an hour or so without boiling over. Owen Parcher remembered newspaper photographs of cars parked off to the side of the road, hoods open, radiators steaming, unhappy-looking women holding up whatever would shade them from the New Mexico sun — newspapers, articles of clothing, and even a few parasols. There was a flat turn-off area halfway up the hill, so Owen, just to be sure, pulled over to let his more improved 1946 engine cool down for a while.

He and his cousin, Sims Summerville, had been a week on the road from Philadelphia, headed to the Summerville School on the edge of the Santa Fe foothills. They were both newly discharged from active service in the war, Owen a young officer in the OSS offices in London and Sims a general's aide-de-camp in the military bureaucracy, also in London. They had met several times in the war years, renting rooms in the city and country inns to get away and talk about their family.

Both their families were ill at ease about the move west. Painting and writing were not proper endeavors, but it was assumed that good sense would eventually fall like gentle rain upon the two, so no sort of intervention was needed.

Owen's father Isaac was, indeed, a kind man, not forcing his son into a life he hated, and he was the one who circulated the good-sense theory at family gatherings. If not sure in his heart that it was so, he proceeded on that basis. He was an avid reader of Greek history and admired those leaders who reigned during difficult times with forbearance and patience, waiting until the citizens came themselves to the wanted conclusion. Forcing the unruly only hardened their stance, so Isaac felt comfortable playing out the lead, betting strongly that Owen and Sims would return in time to the fold in the upper reaches of Philadelphia, maybe even back to take over their family houses.

Owen, for his part, played along. He remembered his mother laughing when he said he wanted to paint paintings. *What nonsense,* she said at the family dinner, *just like your cousin Sims's telling me he wanted to be a novelist. Such foolish boys.* Augustine was able to scare the boys when they were young, but she was not aware how strong their backbones had become during the war years. If they appeared much the same on the outside, agreeable and handsome young scions, there was an invincible core waiting inside each of them.

Highway 66 was the best route across America then and the boys who were now men spent a day or two getting to Chicago. They then wove themselves down through the corn and wheat center of the country, arriving at last to the southernmost part of the Rocky Mountains. Owen had seen the school property only once before, on a family trip west to visit his Aunt Malvina. Some memories were unclear, but he did recall how exotic it was, how different from his life back home.

The buildings in Santa Fe were said to be made of mud bricks, cooler in the summer heat, and he particularly remembered the odd silence of the bedroom he was assigned. He could barely hear people talking in nearby rooms, only a slight wordless murmur. Malvina told him that it was only one of the many secrets to houses made out of the earth, secrets as old as time. Now this Summerville School, with its hidden joys, was his.

"Are you nervous about finally getting here?" Sims asked as they waited inside the auto, hood up above the hot engine. He opened the car door for a breeze and to stretch out his long legs.

"Yes, kind of. Malvina and Alberta took the train east a few days ago, so it will be empty. I think there is a caretaker looking after it all."

"What do you expect?"

"Malvina left everything. Furnishings, books, dinner services, silverware, glassware, sheets, towels, garden tools, and even three cars in the garage. It was part of the deal."

"Almost like she died and left the estate. What about the people who worked for her?"

"She gave all her staff a retirement bonus, so we're starting from scratch. She said I should hire whomever I want. Maybe only a housekeeper-cook and a gardener. I remember there was a large lawn, lots of flower borders, and a walled vegetable garden, which neither of us want to spend our own time on. Father, always the man behind the desk, said I must not let everything go to seed, since the property was a family investment as well as mine. And neither of us wants to cook."

"I like the idea of letting it all go, tumbleweeds growing in the lawn, paint peeling from the trim, and curtains splitting in the sun like at Miss Havisham's house. In five years, I'll have the novel finished and you will be on your way to a first museum exhibit, and we'll have beards, dirty fingernails, and tanned skin. The neighbors will be too afraid to come by. I'll be wearing buckskin and high boots, and you will have a black beret and a Paisley foulard. The family friends will ask timidly about us back home, are they doing well, and your mother will say, 'No, indeed. The boys have gone to rack and ruin. Just like Malvina. That place called Santa Fe turns everybody bad.'"

"Mother has strong opinions," Owen said.

"She told my mother we'd be back by next spring and at work for the family, tails between our legs. Does that make your blood boil?"

"Decidedly. I think the radiator is not boiling now. Let's get going."

Without further automotive worries, they reached the crest of the La Bajada escarpment, a long volcanic flow with black boulders and piñon trees strewn down along the south-facing slopes. A few miles' drive across the flat summit until, at last, there was a view across the next valley to Santa Fe, nestled in the foothills up against a high range of mountains. Early snow topped the tallest peaks, but the town below was flecked with gold. Both of the men were silent as they approached the town. It was a still day, and as they got closer they could see smoke from the chimneys going straight up and dissolving. A thin cloud of haze centered over it all.

Skipping the first road in, they took the second road. It wound down through arroyos with chamisa shrubs and small juniper trees until the first houses appeared, close to the road, flat-roofed and all earthen-colored. As they closed in on the center of town, houses and shops lined the road, a few people walked along the road. Owen stopped at the Esso gas station near the state capitol building to fill up the tank and to ask the way across town.

"You turn right here for Summerville School," the attendant said, "then in a quarter mile, go right on Canyon Road. I hope you're not selling textbooks. That school's been closed for several years."

"No, I'm a painter and Sims here is a writer."

"Santa Fe has plenty of those already."

"Maybe not good ones."

"I guess we'll see."

"What's your name? I'm Owen Parcher."

"Hank Garcia. Good to meet you. Sorry, I sound more like a smartass than I am."

"We'll be back for gas. Thanks, Hank."

"Good luck with the painting and writing."

After the Canyon Road turn, Owen thought that he remembered the way there. Farther up to the right, then along beside the river for a while and he saw the front gateposts next to a gnarled old cottonwood in pale-yellow leaf, many leaves fallen across the gateway. The drive circled the green lawn around to the house that Owen remembered as the main house. The warm day had turned to cool and the smell of piñon fires from nearby houses was a new sensation to both of them, an exotic, almost Asian incense foretelling of unfamiliar events awaiting.

"It's grander than I thought it would be," Sims said.

"Welcome to our new home, my love," Owen said as he stopped the car, leaning over with a broad smile to give his cousin a long kiss on the mouth.

NOT SO SPICY, PLEASE

It was a month later, the men settling into their new life. Owen had taken over the school's art studio as his own, a single easel where there had been a dozen before, and a north-facing window that slanted just slightly inwards. The other easels, desks, and chairs had been taken to a storage building and the tired old linen draperies consigned to the trash. Sunlight came in through the south windows, but his easel was placed next to the northern light. There was a medium-sized canvas on his easel, with the adjoining paint table arrayed with two lines of oil paint in tubes. The aroma of turpentine was strong, as he had just washed his brushes from a day of work.

Owen decided early on that he would try to find his way as a modernist painter, spurning the motifs he had seen on visits to the academy back in Philadelphia. He and the students he talked to were convinced that the way forward was through non-objective paintings, canvases that tried to mirror the ephemeral ill-ease and malaise that many men felt after going to war. The landscape around Santa Fe was of no interest, nor were the Pueblo Indians that the other painters in town had in their focus since the turn of the century. There would be no braves in a seated circle illuminated from below by the embers of a teepee fire. These old motifs were passé, not what young American painters strived for. Owen's first pieces were experimental — sharp parallel lines meeting banks of curving lines. The new against the primordial. He saw them as the frontier between the old and what was yet to come. He was excited by the results, planning larger canvases in his mind.

Sims had searched around the school grounds and found a small cottage with only a single sitting room, small kitchen, and smaller bath. He took the bed, side-tables, and straight chairs to the storage building. It now had only a good-sized writing table and chair, a pair of green-shaded student lamps, and an upholstered reading chair with a standing lamp. Books stood in small piles against the wall. Sims was equally committed to the modernist movement, no historical cowpuncher sagas or coming-of-age stories. His first pages were stacked up beside the typewriter in what he described to Owen as a broken-image tale. The finished novel could be rearranged like a cracked mirror on the wall of a room, adjoining pieces reflecting quite different parts of the room. It was like shuffling Tarot cards. Afterwards he would write small linking passages, to make one part glide into another.

There were French novels written that way, not plotted with one action bringing on the next, but an overhead view of a group of lives, episodes from here and there in time. He could well be an omniscient giant over a group of houses, lifting their roofs, looking down at what was going on. The minds of various characters were there to be entered, spilling their thoughts for the readers.

With these winds of modernism swirling about the two men, they felt in their hearts that they were part of the new, even if they were not in New York or Paris. The subject of what was modern and how to create it in the middle of America came up in conversations over almost every meal. What was a modern painting or how did you define a modern novel, the new way? New messages and stories needed new techniques.

And the solution to these meals had been solved in the first days after arrival. The couple who had worked for Malvina came by to welcome the men to Santa Fe, hoping a continuance of their paychecks from the new owners. Rita and Perfecto Sanchez had worked nowhere else in their lives, so they knocked with hope on the front door of the main house.

Owen came to the door and invited them to come in and sit down. He asked, "Do you think the two of you can maintain the grounds and cook our meals? We are just two men to look after instead of a whole school with teachers and unruly students."

Rita, just barely over five feet tall, was the more assertive of the two, saying, "Miss Summerville was a good woman to work for. Perfecto can take care of the grounds with some extra help now and then, and I am fine in the kitchen alone. I will need extra help only if you have parties. We have many cousins for those."

"I have heard good things about your meals. Do you remember me from my visit here about fifteen years ago?"

"Yes, for sure. You choked and cried on my red chile enchilada."

"Let's start again with the red chile. Maybe not so spicy at first."

"I understand."

"I think Sims and I will be easy to work for. What did Malvina pay you?"

"Both Perfecto and me were paid the same, twenty dollars a week. Miss Summerville said women should get the same as men."

"Would twenty-five dollars a week for each of you be satisfactory?"

"Very much. We'll be happy to continue here with the family."

"Can you start tomorrow?"

"We can, señor. What will you do with all the buildings?"

"Leave most of them vacant for now. I've taken one for a studio, Sims has his own writing house."

Rita took charge immediately, writing out menus and shopping lists. She told them how much money had to be in her kitchen cash account each week, advising that there could be more requests for extras. Owen's allowance from the family came as a check from the family trust offices on the first of each month and Sims's money arrived at the first of every quarter, his banker father haughty about monthly stipends. Neither of the two men were used to hiring a cook and a housekeeper to clean for them, their family households back in Philadelphia running like clockwork because of longtime staffs and tradition. Malvina, when leaving Philadelphia thirty years ago for good, had shown the forethought to check with her mother's cook before heading west and was rewarded with a copy of Pierre Caron's *French Dishes for American Tables,* an early guide to what was possible from the French kitchen. Rita took to continental menus over the years, giving Malvina and Alberta dinners like few others in Santa Fe. The enchiladas, tamales, and chiles remained, but were joined with ragouts, potages, béarnaises and hollandaises, an outpost of continental cuisine in the Santa Fe foothills.

It was with immense luck that the Sanchezes came into the lives of Owen and Sims, a staff fully formed and ready to go to work without training or instruction. They arrived the first day in time for Rita to make lunch and left after the dinner dishes were put away. Perfecto mowed the large lawn that same day, swept the terraces, and raked away the yellow leaves. As the days went on, Rita had only to ask them what time they wanted dinner and the two arrived at a set table with candles. The good life of Summerville, a machine left with only a momentary lull, was going again. Owen realized that he was heavily indebted to his aunt not only for the real property but also for organizing the gentle rhythms of life they were now enjoying.

This night was a New Mexican dinner — fried pork chops, posole, braised squashes, greens, and corn bread. Natillas de leche for dessert. The two men sat across from each other at the sides of one end of the table in the dark-walled dining room, with the glass doors open into the adjoining living room, where a fire was lit in the fireplace on the far wall. Rita had lighted candles in the pair of pottery candelabra, with a bouquet of grasses and dried summer flowers. Owen often wondered at dinner how many other Santa Fe houses were having such refined meals. Were they, in fact, the only ones in town?

"Do you want to have some others over for dinner soon?" he asked Sims. "Say Hank Garcia and his girlfriend, and maybe the neighbor family, the old artist and his wife who live across the way?"

"That would be good, but...Owen, I'm happy with it just being us."

"I know, but I think we need to start to be part of the Santa Fe art scene. Malvina left us a list of people to call."

"Sure. Let's do it this Saturday night. I'll go by and ask Hank tomorrow."

"I'll ask Parthon. It's a good excuse to see his studio."

Rita came in to clear the dishes and they asked what she thought. Saturday nights were when she got out the French cookbook, keeping up the tradition even when it was just dinner for the two men.

"Miss Summerville very much liked Parthon Ellis and his wife. Had them over here for dinner often. I hope the Garcia boy and his girl, whoever she is, won't feel out of place."

"He's our first and best friend, Rita," said Sims. "It wouldn't be right not including him."

Rita said nothing as she raised her eyebrows and wiped the crumbs with an extra vigor. This was the start of the men's egalitarian table, an across-the-board mix of locals that was not duplicated in many other large houses in Santa Fe. Owen more than Sims had a built-in sense that there was an obligation to entertain, probably ingrained in him by his socially prominent mother. But both of them, without discussing it at length, accepted that having others over for dinner was just part of life, part of what made a good life, but not in the way of their parents. The years in the army had shown them the discomforts of a caste system. They would ask guests from both the Anglo and Hispanic lists, with or without pedigrees. It would be an open table at Summerville House.

RED VERMOUTH WITH A LITTLE ICE

S aturday evening came, and Rita had taken on two of her cousins, an older woman to help in the kitchen and a young man to serve at table. Owen was planning to make drinks himself for the guests so Rita set up a cocktail bar on the large side-table of the living room, just as she had in Malvina's time. A handled silver tray held all the liquor bottles, the glasses, a knife, and napkins on the bare wood, dishes of lemons, olives, and toothpicks nearby. Perfecto lit the fire a few minutes before people were to arrive.

"Does this evening pique your sense of humor?" Sims asked Owen.

"Why?"

"We're replicating our parents' lives, hosting society dinners. Husband and wife."

"Why can't it be man and man? Man and lover?"

"I think your Aunt Malvina did that. Woman and woman, take it or leave it."

"It seemed to work."

"We'll see tonight. I still think it is humorous."

Hank Garcia's girlfriend turned out to be more imposing than they could have expected. Viona Maes had a cosmopolitan sense of style, wearing high-waisted ivory linen slacks that tapered out as they went down, a long-sleeved black silk blouse, a string of silver beads the size of large pearls with earrings to match. Her black hair was cut sharply short on an angle and she moved around the room with long steps. Owen was delighted to welcome her. Hank was dressed almost like the two hosts, informal trousers, but a tie and shirt while they both had open-necked shirts.

"I've always wanted to see inside this house," said Viona, after Owen mixed her a red vermouth-and-soda. "Rita wanted me to work for parties when the ladies were here, but I always had something else to do."

"So you're related to Rita," asked Sims.

"Most of the Spanish families in Santa Fe are related, some closer than others. Rita thought I was just being rebellious but I really had other parties to go to. I don't think she knows I was coming tonight."

It was clear to Owen that Hank was very proud of Viona, because he smiled as he watched her walking about checking out paintings and art pieces set on the tables. Owen could not help bringing up the notion that Hank and Viona were more like brother and sister than boyfriend-girlfriend. And there was her mannish quality, despite her graceful movements. She and Hank seemed like co-members of a unisex soccer team, equals more than paramours. It would be a good subject to discuss when he, Sims, and Hank had their threesome dinners during the week.

The Ellises arrived twenty minutes later, Parthon with a heavy overcoat, rubbing his hands from the cold. He was tall and thin, slightly bent with age, a full head of white hair carefully parted and an unmistakable patrician bearing. Sims took his and his wife's coats over to the entryway bench and made introductions to the others. Mona Ellis had none of Viona's sense of style, but a sweet, gracious expression in her pale pink, expensive floor-length dress with ruffles. Owen knew at once she had run a merry dance living with the famous painter, always looking over at parties to see if he was talking too intently with another woman. It was a pattern he had seen in his mother's friends back in Philadelphia, the bright-eyed man with the worried-brow woman. As he mixed the drinks for the newcomers, he knew it was going to be an interesting evening and was proud to think how wrong Rita was about Hank and Viona feeling ill at ease. If anything, they appeared to be more at ease than the Ellises.

Parthon took his drink and walked over to Viona. "Is Santa Fe your home, my dear?" he asked.

"Yes, Mr. Ellis."

"It's Parthon for you."

"I know your paintings. My uncle Octavio, the judge, has a whole wall of them."

"And what do *you* think...of them?"

"Uncle Octavio loves them because he loves the land around Santa Fe. If I were going to buy a painting, I would want it to be very modern. Strong and upsetting. Not lovable."

"Did you learn to talk this way in school?"

"I respect your work, sir, but when the sisters at the Loretto School took us to the museum to see your paintings, I sneaked into the adjoining gallery and saw strange new paintings. Ones with black lines and lightning bolts, circles inside circles, and one with orange zigzags. I don't think any landscape, even yours, could be as exciting as those."

"Rebellious right from the start?"

"Not really."

"I also paint portraits. May I ask you to sit sometime?"

"I would like that, Mr. Parthon."

Mona Ellis came across the room to see what new trouble her husband was brewing. "So what were you two talking so animatedly about?"

"Viona, here, has agreed to sit for a portrait."

"What fun, my dear Viona. We'll plan to have lunch as well."

Parthon said, "It may take more than one session, dearie."

"Several lunches, then."

Owen recognized the familiar ploy, that with lunches she could keep an eye on what was going on in the studio. Poor Mona, he thought, ever keeping the wall of matrimony repaired, cracks needing attention right from the start. He wondered how many repairs had come before, how many young women required successive lunches.

At dinner, Parthon, comfortable with the good points of social discourse, took over the conversation by asking questions of the two new young men in his neighborhood. He first turned his attention to Sims and his novel. Parthon asked, "Tell us about your book."

"An editor friend advised me to never give the story away, but have a sentence ready for just such a question, one that would describe the spirit of the novel and nothing more."

"And that sentence is...?"

"My narrator is a writer who comes home after the war and tries to describe how hard it is to stop the vivid dreams."

"Does he succeed?"

"One sentence only, sir."

"When the time is right, you must show your book to our neighbor, Prestor McCain. Before he retired here after a handsome, I think, family bequest, he was a New York literary agent. I know he likes to keep his hand in on what is new."

"Thanks so much, Parthon."

"And Owen, what can you tell us about your paintings?"

"The same one-sentence approach. I am putting the sounds and sights of war onto canvas."

"I would like to see them sometime, harder to do than your simple sentence would imply. We all sat here in the shady streets of Santa Fe during the war, safely away from danger. Most of us were too old to enlist. I admire you men who served. Let's drink to you."

With that the spotlight shifted to current events, Parthon and Mona keeping their position as entitled captains of the conversation. They said that they were Democrats, as were most of the town's artist families, and within the first half hour, they let the table know where they had gone to school on the East Coast, how many crossings to Europe they had taken, and which high-born families they knew. Owen looked without expression over at Sims, whose look back matched his. The Ellises might as well have been only slightly Bohemian, but well connected, members of their families' friends.

At the end of the evening, Sims took a flashlight and accompanied the Ellises across the street to their adjoining house. Parthon put his hand around Sims's shoulder and said, "I'll let Prestor know about your book, the one you won't talk about."

LA TORMENTA

Winter came in right on schedule to Santa Fe with several severe storms in the first weeks of December. Snow built up in drifts on the north sides of the buildings even though the days between storms were sunny. The front lawn was a blanket of white, but the lane around it had been cleared by Perfecto. It was a Saturday night, when Rita customarily cooked the special French dinner. Owen had early on told Hank Garcia to always plan on Saturday night dinners with them at Summerville House, as a regular pattern. Hank was their first friend in Santa Fe, after all, wisely treating each of them with equal regard. He arrived early for dinner, just as the wind was picking up and the snowfall turned to heavy flakes. For an easy departure, he parked his pickup truck just beyond the front door.

Summerville House was built to a traditional East Coast or Territorial plan, a long entrance hall or sala in the middle of the house, two pairs of rooms entering from each side. The sitting room was the first archway to the left, with a dining room through French doors beyond that. The next door from the hall led to a smaller library, with pantries and kitchen farther on. On the right were four bedrooms, all entered from a perpendicular hallway down the middle. There were two smaller bedrooms on the back side, sharing a bathroom, and two larger bedrooms with an adjoining door facing the lawn, with their own bathrooms.

In her trips around New Mexico, Malvina had collected many items of Pueblo art to decorate the house and all of these she left in place in her sale to the trust. The dining room sideboard had above it a long row of Hopi kachinas. First-Phase Chief's blankets from Navajo with their black-and-white stripes hung on the walls of the sitting room like contemporary canvases, large pots from many pueblos were on the chests and pedestals in the sala and the other rooms.

Interspersed everywhere were small paintings by Malvina's artist friends — canyons, dances, landscapes, clouds, portraits, abstracts — all about twelve inches square in thin gold frames. Many had small lights over them, so the house at night was lit with an ambient golden glow reflected from art. The table lamps had parchment shades faded to light sienna, adding a deeper tone to the rooms. Without discussing it, Rita each night turned on all the separate electric lights and Perfecto laid and lit the fireplace. They tended the complex machine that was Summerville House, making it look simple.

Since Owen and Sims had moved in, the two men took for their own the two larger bedrooms on the front of the house. Sims regularly spent the night in Owen's bed, however, mussing up the sheets in his own room in a continuing effort to fool Rita. The two men believed that Rita knew the truth, and wondered if Owen's aunt and her lover used the same bit of deception. To avoid embarrassment on either side, it was just as well to keep up the ruse. Since Rita arrived just before noon, there was little chance of her finding the men still asleep together. In the world of 1946, it was not thought that two men could sleep together with impuni-

ty, unless they were young brothers or where large impov-
erished families lived in one house. Still, it annoyed Sims
to play the game, not be truthful. Men ought to be able to
express their love and not have to prevaricate.

The piñon fire in the fireplace was making soft crack-
ling noises in the sitting room. Hank by now felt easy about
entering the house without knocking, so he sat down on the
long leather sofa in front of the fireplace to await the arrival
of his friends from the bedroom wing. The brown leather
sofa was the sort that appeared to be upholstered over river
rocks, small round cushions covering the whole piece with
a brass nail head at each intersection. Even though it looked
vastly uncomfortable, Hank knew you could sink right in.
He always chose it to sit upon, because he directly faced
the fireplace.

He also knew he had been given a lucky stroke to meet
Owen and Sims that day they arrived, and they were becoming the sort of friends who felt comfortable keeping
silent for stretches rather than filling the air with chatter.
Owen had a calm sturdiness, Hank thought, the sort that
could be depended on in a fire or a flood. He would know
what to do. And Hank admired Owen's manly constitution,
broad shoulders and long back, legs close to the ground, the
stout sort that Hank's father said you wanted working with
you in the fields. Tall poets with delicate hands were of no
use on the land. And Owen was the first friend who had fair
hair, the color of corn tassels. Both Owen and Sims had
blue eyes, not a common sight in Santa Fe.

Sims was the tall poet, the one with more pepper in his
soul, always trying to make a joke out of any situation. He
was taller than Owen or Hank, with runner's long legs and
arms. Hank noticed he walked with his feet straight ahead,

no angling out. He wondered if Sims learned that in boarding school, or the military, or if he just came that way. Sims
had dark brown hair, not black like his. If somebody had
made Hank choose between the two, he could not.

They both held a sensual allure for Hank, a secret he
knew he ought to confess to them soon. He was not sure
how or when, but he had often heard his father saying that
a good man always tells others his inner thoughts. They
would come out eventually, so it was better to make the
time your own.

His reveries were interrupted with Owen and Sims arriving together.

"A real *tormenta*, Hank," Owen said. "Are Santa Fe
winters usually like this?"

"Not this early. Usually late January or February."

"I think we should all escape to Barbados or Jamaica,"
Sims said. "You can tell the gas station that we kidnapped
you."

"I would love that, but Uncle Gilbert couldn't make it
without me. Whether I want it or not, I am sure Gilbert will
leave me the gas station in his will. I'm a grease monkey
for life."

"I was kidding."

Rita had gone home early to miss the deep snow, she and
Perfecto walking the few blocks to their house. She set out
a buffet for the men, kept warm in covered dishes on stands
over votive candles. At the end of the sideboard was a stack
of plates, also kept warm over votive candles, and serving
spoons. The table settings were in place with candelabra lit.
Obviously, Rita had done this before on winter nights.

The world of writers and painters was foreign to Hank,
but he knew it should be taken seriously. Santa Fe had be-

come a sanctuary for such people, with ties to New York, Europe, and beyond. The local families talked about them as if they were curiosities, odd ones who arrived from elsewhere with endless stores of money. Part of their money must have come from writing and painting, Hank thought. At dinner, he asked the men to describe what they were doing.

"I've nearly got my novel done, Hank. It is basically written and I am trying to splinter it and rearrange it, to make the reading more interesting."

"I don't understand why straight on is not better than splintered."

"Think about a cracked mirror," answered Sims. "Aren't the reflections more exciting? The floor is reflected on a piece next to a piece with the ceiling. The far wall melting into the near wall. It makes the reader work a little, ponder the parts of my story. It is like a puzzle with only parts of it assembled, the whole just a bit beyond our sight."

"You describe it so well, Sims. I'll have to read it when you're done and see if I understand. And, Owen, I think you're going the same way with your paintings."

"Somewhat. Neither of us wanted to do work like artists did before the war. Some in New York even want a clean sweep, nothing the same. I still use the old forms in a new way...patterns that say what I want. Abstract patterns."

"So, will both of you make a lot of money? Is what you do what everybody wants?"

"We'll see," Sims said. "There were times when groups of artists and writers got together in one place and wonderful new work came out. Paris after the First World War, the Bloomsbury Group in England, Florence and Rome in the fifteenth century, the Transcendentalists in New England. Impressionism in France in the late nineteenth century brought new paintings, writings, and even music together. Maybe Santa Fe can be like those."

"What about the old painters and writers who have been here for the last thirty years? Will they change like you?"

"Again, we'll see," Sims said. "I think new younger people have to come here. From what I've seen of the Old Guard here, like Parthon Ellis, they are set in their ways. Not looking for modernism."

"Well, I better go. Snow is getting real deep out there."

"Stay here, Hank," Owen said. "You can have Sims's bed, and he can sleep with me. He usually does, anyway."

Hank thought about it for a moment, and said, "I would like to stay, but I need to call Gilbert. He would worry."

Sims said, "Tell him we will keep you warm and happy."

"That might scare him, really make him worry."

After Hank made his call, they walked onto the front portal to assess the storm. Hank's pickup had all but disappeared under a mound of white, and the snow was still pounding down with large icy flakes. The men blew out the candles in the dining room, turned off the electric lights, and showed Hank where he would stay, disappearing through the adjoining door into the far front bedroom.

NOW I LAY ME DOWN

Sims put on his pajamas and found another pair for Hank. Of course, the legs were too long, so he got down on his knees and rolled them up. Both the men broke into laughter at the sight of the result.

"Good night, Bud," Sims said. "You'll probably hear Owen snoring through the door. I've learned to sleep through it anyway."

Sims walked through and closed the door adjoining the other bedroom. Hank was excited, not even close to sleep. He heard nothing except for the hushed fall of snow outside, the wind picking up at times with a soft whistle. Gilbert had sounded unhappy on the phone, but Hank told him he would be home first thing in the morning, in time to make his breakfast. They would go together to the gas station.

Trying to calm his racing thoughts, he replayed their conversations about art and modernism at dinner, look-ing for patches he understood. Words came easily to Sims, probably because he was a writer. Owen was harder to read, a painter concerned with what he saw rather than heard. They were a good pair, Hank decided, not in end-less competition over their art, one trying to be better than the other. He wondered if two writers could live together, always talking into the late hours, or two painters, never having much to say. A painter and a writer could make a happy life. Finally his mind slowed down and the darkness of sleep took over.

It was almost morning, because there was a light violet glow on the snow over the lawn. Sims touched his shoulder.

"Come to bed with us."

Sims led him by the arm through the door and motioned for Hank to get into the open bedcovers before him. It was warm in their bed. Sims slipped in behind him.

Hank thought Owen was still asleep in front of him when Sims came close and wrapped himself around. Hank became full awake and erect, feeling Sims's hands now caressing his chest under the pajama top. He hoped Sims would continue.

Hank started to talk but Sims put his hand lightly over his mouth and said, "Hush, my love."

Owen came awake and moved closer. Hank could smell him, not unpleasant but full of sensual sleep. Owen kissed Hank, a deep thrust. Hank wondered if he would explode with Sims nibbling the back of his neck and shoulder. Somehow, their night-clothes were slipped off and Hank passed his hands over the firm skin of both men. In the joy, Hank wondered if these two had done this before, or was it as new to them as it was to him? He put his hand gently over on Owen's erection and he knew that Owen was as excited as he was. How could life be any better than this? Was this what exaltation was? How could three men come together this way? His thoughts became wordless in the rush, skin moving across skin, and what was an hour of love seemed like only a minute.

The night turned to morning, a band of sunlight came right across the snowfield, through the windows and onto the men. Sims had a small cloth, washing both of the others. It was cold in the room.

As he washed Hank he said, "Now that was a good lay."

Owen smiled in agreement.

Hank did not know how to talk about what had happened. It had been so joyful for him, he thought everything now was going to go downhill. Maybe that was what life was, a climb to the top peak of joy and slide down afterwards, lower and lower, never to happen again.

Owen sensed Hank's unease and said, "A door opened for all of us, Hank. Can there be a life together for the three of us? How does that work?"

"I don't know," Hank said. "It was so great I can't talk about it."

"I'll go make us some coffee," Sims said. "We can talk then."

Sims thought how odd it was that the sex between the three of them had gone so well, so exciting, and now in the light of day it was impossible to talk about it. The quick flash of a thought occurred to him that maybe sex, the loving touch, was the only true communication, the only truthful way to converse with one you love. It was a superior language that words could never supplant, a book within a book. Words were so pale in the morning light. He had loved Owen so completely that he never thought this was possible. Rather than putting it aside, not talking about it, Sims knew that this was their future. The three of them together. Somehow, it *would* work.

"No," Hank said, "I need to go make breakfast for Gilbert."

"Call us later."

"Okay."

Reality started to come back as Hank swept the heavy snow off his pickup. What was he doing? He could not make a secret life with these two from the upper class without him always at the low end of the triangle. What would his family say, his brother, the uncles, and many cousins of the extended clan, when they found out? He could think of nobody in his family who was like him, so he would have to hide from them all. The pickup started right up and sledged through the deep snow around the snow-covered lawn and out to the street. At least he knew Gilbert would not ask questions, always giving Hank a comfortable privacy.

The Garcia house was only a few blocks away, a three-room adobe cottage. Hank's father's house was next door, but it was no longer his. Hank, a small boy, moved one house away and thereafter he considered Uncle Gilbert's house as his home. He was accustomed to making their breakfast, so he went quickly at it while Gilbert sat at the table. After he placed the plates with scrambled eggs and sausage on the kitchen table, both men started to eat, with no conversation.

Gilbert broke their customary silence. "It is good you have Anglo friends as well as the local boys. I want the best for you."

"I like Owen and Sims, and admire what they do."

"You could do other things, too. Other than our gas station."

"I'm happy working with you, Uncle."

"You should go to college, learn to be a lawyer or doctor."

"It's not for me, Gilbert."

Gilbert picked their plates up and washed them in the sink. He said, "I see the world changing quickly now, after the war. When my own uncles came back from the first war, they had seen too much. They both married but were never happy here in Santa Fe, knowing there was another world out there. They thought they were trapped here in backward Santa Fe, when the rest of the world was going ahead."

"But I don't feel trapped."

"I'm afraid you will, and I don't want that."

"I love you, uncle."

Hank knew that Gilbert knew more than he was saying. He had always seen into his nephew's thoughts, knowing when to suggest they talk about them. Hank could not talk about this with Gilbert just now. He wondered if he ever could. It was good to have someone to share your thoughts, but it could also be uncomfortable.

A PALE FERN-GREEN

Malvina and Alberta persevered until they found a second-hand, light-gray Hispano-Suizza in a London showroom, an English family disposing with the costly fripperies of a now-dead uncle, a find in the garages of his Hampshire country house. The salesman said that this was the last and best of his six-car horde. On the appointed day after their purchase, they drove to Dover for the ferry across the Channel.

After the drive through a rainy Normandy, the sun came out. With the top down most of the way afterwards, they skirted around Paris on the small roads and reached Avignon in the south of France by the first of December, a sunny warm day. Alberta had picked up a collection of silk scarves from shops along the way, securely tying down her broad-brimmed hat under the chin with two of them knotted together. Malvina's similar hat was kept from flying away less fashionably with a leather thong. Word spread among the hotelkeepers in small towns along their way of the two rich Americans, heading south. Few failed to notice them as the gray machine whizzed down the back roads through the small villages, geese and chickens scurrying out of its way, tales kept alive of their passing-through for many days afterwards.

It took a week of driving east along the country roads from Avignon through Aix-en-Provence, Grasse, Antibes, Nice to their destination just before the Italian border, Menton. Malvina had read a real estate ad in a copy of *Country Life* during their stay in London, a small fine estate for sale in the finest winter weather in all of France — Menton. The ad said the stone main house had three outbuildings, six terraces with citrus and olives, and was in need of "some" restoration. Malvina spoke a schoolgirl French, suitable to engaging rooms and ordering meals, but she felt uneasy trying to converse about real estate on the telephone. So they must just go see for themselves what this advertisement offered.

They knew as they approached Menton why it was an internationally known, agreeable climate. The Alpes Maritime came very close to the Mediterranean at this point, like a tall heat-reflecting wall facing south, protected from cold north winds. French roads had not been repaired so much in this area outside of the German occupation, so Malvina drove slowly over potholes as they approached the ochre-colored town. The agent who had run the ad, a *M. d'Effron,* had an office right on the main square, a sign claiming that English was spoken. He looked up from his desk to Malvina brandishing a copy of the magazine, open to the ad circled in dark ink.

"Why would two American ladies like this old house?" he asked.

"For the peace and tranquility. It has a good garden, does it not?" Malvina asked.

"After the Great War it was one of the best."

"And now?"

"*Malheursement*, it is showing its age."

"Does the studio you describe here have good light?"

"It was the home of Pierre Frejus, a painter not so well known now. He painted fine pieces there, many now on the upper floors of our own *l'Hotel de Ville*. His widow is selling, sad to be moving in with her sister in Paris."

"May we see it now?"

"Today? Right now? I must telephone."

Malvina and Alberta waited outside on a bench, but could hear the long, animated conversation through the open window. M. d'Effron came to the door, now with overcoat and hat, and asked the ladies to follow his Citroen, parked nearby. The property for sale was just beyond the town on a hillside road called the *Impasse de la Maison Russe*.

It was a two-story, south-facing stone house, pale-yellow stucco falling away in places, with aging wooden shutters at each window and door. The windows were regularly spaced across the second story, seven of them. All the painted surfaces were peeling, much gray wood exposed. The house had a smell of wood smoke and cooking. The main studio was a single, large room with a many-paned window facing north, smaller windows facing south. It had high a ceiling of adzed oak beams, very similar to the studio back at the Summerville School, but larger and more refined.

Alberta said nothing, but Malvina could see she was delighted. There was a smaller studio as well, and a cottage. The citrus and olive trees needed pruning, pathways crowded with overgrown rosemary shrubs, fragrant as they brushed by. The four hectares descended the hill in a series of terraces, faced with rough stone. A swimming pool, surrounded by overgrown orange trees on the lowest terrace, was dry, with a layer of rotted leaves and a row of desiccated wood chairs. Altogether, it was just exactly what Malvina had hoped for, a restoration project of several years for her and a handsome painting studio for Alberta to retreat to while the refurbishing work continued.

Madame Frejus spoke no English, so Malvina, not trusting her rudimentary French, discussed the price with M. d'Effron. Thirty thousand francs, or about five thousand dollars. With an experienced eye, Malvina knew it would cost the same to refurbish it all. The total price was a twentieth of what she had received from the sale of the Summerville School. She said to all of them in the room, "*Il est parfait,*" and shook hands with Madame, who hugged Alberta, both of them crying and laughing at the same time. Malvina saw no need to even ask for a price reduction.

After a week of fine-pointed negotiations about the exact property lines and paperwork with a *notaire* in the center of Menton, the house was theirs, the sellers accepting with delight the personal check with Malvina's bold signature, her ability to pay such a price verified through a succession of bank calls across the Atlantic and whispers from the translators. Since Madame Frejus's sister had a fully equipped household in a Paris suburb, the removal people needed to pack only a few of the more favorite furnishings to be sent along with the widow. She was saying goodbye to the south of France and all it had meant.

Thus, for the delighted purchasers, the house was almost completely furnished, ready to occupy, a happy surprise. Dishes, cooking pieces, lamps, books, linens, a sea-green Deux Cheveux Citroen in working order, but no silverware. Alberta said to Malvina, "I love our being on a street called a Russian Impasse. Much lovelier sounding than a Soviet Dead End. It will be fun to tell your brother's sister-in-law we have come to a dead end, just as she had anticipated."

"You should leave her alone, Alberta. Augustine can't help it."

"Always too much fun. Of course, Augustine can help it."

Malvina got right into the repair work, taking M. d'Effron's suggestions for construction workers and craftsmen. Her English-to-French dictionary did not have many of the terms she needed, but she was a quick study with the men. They immediately knew this was not an ordinary woman, but someone who knew what she was talking about in building matters, who needed to be paid attention to. The stucco was repaired, shutters and doors painted a pale fern-green, trees trimmed, pathways restored, studio windows washed, heavy plate silverware from the now shuttered *Hotel Splendide* purchased in a local shop, and an appointment made by letter several months away with the very busy swimming pool expert who had to come all the way from Nice. Life in the house was getting grander and grander, so Alberta ordered up a sign for their gatepost, *La Grande Impasse,* in cursive letters with embellishments.

Among the many workmen who passed through the house, Malvina noticed a thin young man named Guy Martel. He was an able workman, living up to his name, which meant "hammer", but different from the rest in several ways. He wanted to learn English, often asking Malvina the words for the various types of work he was doing, she doing the same, asking for the word in French. He also wanted to know about the house and studio, what sort of painting Alberta did, where they lived in the States, how could a place like New Mexico be one of the states, and so on. As work was winding down on the house, Malvina asked him if he wanted to stay on after the construction work was done.

"What would I do?" he asked her.

"Everything, Martel. You can help keeping the house going. Paint the shutters when they need it. Work in the potager. Drive us to town. Keep the automobile going and full of gasoline. Bring firewood into the house and make the fires. Everything to make our household work that Alberta and I do not want to do. Every fine house has a good man like you at its center. I dislike the word butler, and you would be doing everything he would do and more. Our indispensable man."

"I would like that, Mademoiselle. How much will you pay?"

"Quite a bit more than we paid you to plaster walls and lay stone. This is a position of honor."

"An honor for me. What sort of uniform would I wear?"

"None. A simple pair of black trousers and a white, cotton shirt. We will pay for them. This will not be a palatial household, but an honest one."

"*Mais, oui. Un ménage Americain.*"

"And your first assignment is to learn how to make the perfect dry Martini."

"Dry Martini?"

"Tonight I will show you. Pay close attention."

RUSTLING ROWS OF CORN

I t was the middle of summer after a dry spring, the grasses and plants around Summerville House suffering from lack of rain. The monsoons were said by the weather officials to begin shortly, a line of storms angling northeast from the Pacific bringing tropical moisture far from its home. It was still in the early morning when the three men set off for a drive north, Owen driving the Packard with the top down, Sims in the rumble seat and Hank on the passenger side.

Just north of Santa Fe, the road dropped in altitude through sere barrancas and juniper dry-lands. As they turned west on the road to the pueblo, Hank knew that the sight of the brooding Black Mesa to the right of the highway meant that they were almost to the pueblo, then along a bumpy dirt track they arrived in the central plaza of San Ildefonso Pueblo, his mother's ancestral home. A massive cottonwood shaded the plaza, which was surrounded by two-story mud houses. Owen parked the car to the side of the plaza and they proceeded on foot to the other end.

"Mother's sister lives with their mother just beyond that tallest adobe house," Hank said, pointing the direction. "I haven't been here for a while, but they will welcome us."

The house was a single story, attached to others that were two and three levels high. Sims could see telephone and electrical wires coming from a leaning power pole on the backside of the house, but otherwise it could have been a dwelling from the tenth century. There were no lights by the slatted-wood door, painted a light shade of sky-blue, peeling in places. A wooden rack stood beside the front door of Hank's family house with drying herbs, peppers, and sections of squash on cords like large necklaces.

Hank did not knock but opened the door and said something the other two men could not understand. A middle-aged woman in a white dress came to greet him. She had short-cut dark hair with strands of white and a simple necklace of beads. They hugged and looked at each other for several seconds, holding hands.

"Auntie Clara, these are my new friends, Owen and Sims."

She nodded and smiled and turned sideways to welcome them into the house. It was dark and cool inside, fragrant with unfamiliar aromas and what Sims thought was smoke from burning cedar logs. The room had a back door open onto a garden encircled in a high adobe wall. It was still shady on that side of the house and an old woman sat on a bench with her back to the house. The garden was planted with tall rows of corn, tendrils of squash coming forward into the band of dry dirt between the garden and the house.

Hank leaned down and kissed the old woman on the cheek. She put her hands up on either side of his face, softly saying words in the pueblo language. He sat down on the bench next to her, holding her hand.

"These are my friends, Owen and Sims. Owen is a painter and Sims is a writer of novels. They are very important to me, so I wanted them to meet my San Ildefonso family."

"So..." she said.

Clara brought white-and-turquoise folding chairs from the house and they sat in a half-circle around the old woman, in the shade with the bright sunlit ground just behind them. Clara returned carrying a tray with bottles of orange soda and a plate piled high with small apricot and prune pies. Owen knew that the polite exchanges of Anglo society were not appropriate here, and Sims realized the same, both men staying quiet, occasionally smiling as the old woman looked at them in turn, then looked down. They looked down as well.

"Auntie Clara is a potter," Hank said, breaking the long silence. "Her pots are treasured here on the pueblo, and she lets some be sold to collectors who drive out from Santa Fe."

"May I see some?" Sims asked.

"On your next visit," Clara replied.

The small group sat together for fifteen minutes more, mostly not looking at one another, drinking occasionally from the soda bottles and eating the sweet pies. In the pueblo language Hank said a few sentences to the women, who did not respond. The old grandmother several times gazed for long seconds at Owen and then at Sims, looking down afterwards. Sims thought the silence was not threatening, or ominous, as it well could be. He wondered why that was, why such lack of sociability felt welcoming, open-handed. A breeze came through the corn patch, making rustling noises and there was the buzz of bees around the squash blossoms. Otherwise all was silence.

As Hank rose to signal for them all to depart, Sims resisted the notion to bow ceremonially with palms together, as if they were leaving a Buddhist holy person. With his writer's curiosity, Sims looked around as they walked back through the darkened house, seeing a wood stove in the center with a stove-pipe up to the logged ceiling, a narrow bed with a striped blanket against the wall, a single light-bulb from the ceiling, a few wooden chairs, and a humming General Electric refrigerator in the corner with its high crown of coils. The twentieth century had made some few inroads, but otherwise they were departing a house from very long ago.

Driving back south again, this time with Hank at the wheel, he said, "Thanks for being patient with my family. They are dear to me. I came to stay here after my mother and father died, for about a half-year. I learned to like it."

"I can see why you did," Sims said. "The garden of corn rows appealed to me. And your grandmother is so wrinkled and small, so beautiful."

"She liked both of you. I'm so glad."

"How on earth," Sims said, "could you tell?"

"Trust me, you would know if she did not."

"I thought I could sense approval."

"Grandmother is from the Bluebird Clan. There were two plazas not so long ago, one for the North kiva and one for the South. My mother said there was much fighting back and forth between them when she was a girl, but they patched it all up, took down houses to make a large single plaza. About three hundred now live on the pueblo. Clara says I can always come to live there, no matter what."

"What a great feeling, to always have a place to go," Owen said.

"I don't feel I can always go back to Philadelphia," Sims said.

"I wish I could marry both of you," Hank said, "and then you would forever have a safe pueblo home with me if times got hard."

"I can see it now," Sims said. "Grandmother, dear, please say hello to my two husbands. It's the wonderful new way in the outside world."

"You make fun, Sims. But I really wish that."

"I would love to be one of your husbands, Hank," Owen said.

"Me, too," Sims said, "and summers full of your grandmother's apricot pies."

The storms arrived as they again passed by Black Mesa, so they stopped to pull up the canvas top, now the three of them side-by-side in the front. Hank told them how the San Ildefonso people were major players in the Pueblo Revolt and held out many months in the following Reconquest, giving up only when there was no more water on top of the mesa. And the Spanish afterwards never looked at a San Ildefonso person without wondering if there was a knife or sharp rock hidden in the buckskin trousers. They were not merely simple, agreeable farmers.

"So how did your San Ildefonso mother meet your Santa Fe father?" Sims asked.

"They were working together on a big house restoration in the Nambé valley. An East Coast heiress bought the ruined old two-story hacienda on the river and she had plenty of money to restore it authentically. Dad was a finish carpenter, worked on the fancy ceilings and the trim around doors. Mom was one of those hired to do the mud plaster, like all the women learned at the pueblo. No trowels, all by hand. She said the cacique decided that all the women working together had to be from the Bluebird clan and their pay should be given to him first. He would then parcel it out, keeping a bit for himself. Mom said Dad was the most handsome of the carpenters and she fell at once in love."

"What did their parents think about it?"

"Both sets of parents hated it when they were courting. Tried to prevent them from seeing each other, both sides."

"And how long before they broke away?"

"Not long. They drove to stay at La Fonda in Taos and got married after a short stay. Mother was always quick to say they had separate rooms until they were married."

"But their families must have eventually relented."

"Not entirely. Lots of snide remarks, since both sides felt betrayed. But both families accepted me entirely, the second generation was not to blame. I moved in with Uncle Gilbert after the accident and then with Clara and Grandmother Maria on the pueblo side. I went back and forth, summers at the pueblo to learn to speak some of the Tewa language, the rest of the time in Santa Fe for school."

"It was a hard time for you, I know. You're a brave man."

"Not brave really. Gilbert said I became like a river rock in those years. Smooth on the surface, but hard underneath."

"A hardness of which we are both very fond."

WINCHESTER CATHEDRAL

I t was a cold, foggy January in 1944, all of Britain in
hushed preparation for D-Day, and twenty-two-year-old
Lieutenant Owen Parcher was walking towards the Ritz
Hotel to meet his cousin Lieutenant Sims Summerville,
also twenty-two, for cocktails and lunch. Neither of them
had been to the Ritz before, but Owen's mother Augustine
had written that they should meet there, where she and her
sisters had stayed on their junior year Grand Tour. He must
write back a description of how things looked at what she
said was the most beautiful dining room in all of London.
Since he was early for their meeting, he waited for Sims in
the Long Gallery.

Owen was now well settled in his office at the OSS
Headquarters in London, a former townhouse on Eaton
Square. Despite the fine, white-columned exterior, there
was no sense of luxury in the refitted mansion, desks in
rows across the former grand salon, the finely paneled walls
repainted a pale green as a background for the large map
of all of Europe, England, and North Africa. Living quarters were in the adjoining, lesser houses. Owen was an analyst for this secret outfit, scanning through dispatches from
agents all over the war zone. He had arrived in London half

a year earlier on a troop ship jammed with soldiers headed for the invasion.

The OSS plucked out the men with an Ivy-League background from the rosters of arriving troops, mirroring the English system of trusting the upper class with full and unquestioned access to state secrets. Top-secret clearances would follow. Owen's immediate superior, Major Peter Arrowsmith, was also a Princeton man. He gave Owen a two-week tutorial in the secret operations with another week of target practice on a submachine gun in the country and the use of explosives. Arrowsmith assigned Owen the oversight of agents along the southern border of Occupied France, from his desk in London. The border had been moved south several times, so agents had to move farther south as well, climbing out of Nazi control into the mountains of Spain with only rare radio dispatches.

"Lieutenant Parcher, your table is ready."

The headwaiter, with menus pressed against his chest, escorted him to a far table by the windows, across the elegant pink-and-pale-green marbled dining room. Owen looked out the windows for a park view but the fog pressed against the windows.

Coming in just behind, Sims said as he pulled out the chair, "I have a trip planned for us, that is if you can get a long-weekend pass this next weekend."

"I'm pretty sure."

"A small inn in Winchester, right across from the cathedral. Has a pub attached for food and drink. And a private room upstairs. We can take the train from Waterloo Station...two hours and we're there."

"I'll ask," Owen replied. "Sounds good. But sit down. I have some ideas to discuss."

"About?"

"The future. The war is going to be over soon, and both of us will go back to Philadelphia. You know my father wants me to go to work with him in the factories, and I am sure Borden wants you to go to law school, join the bank."

"He's already written about it," Sims said as their salads arrived.

"Well, I plan a small revolution. Remember, our Grandmother Fairfax left us those small trusts. There is enough in mine to rent a studio and start painting. I want you to live with me there and start your novel. It will be hard to fight the parents, but together we can."

"I don't even need to think about it. Yes."

"I've been writing to Uncle Theodore and he's on our side. He found a large studio way down on Elm Street, three upstairs floors over a grocery in an old stone building. He put a deposit on it and will pay the lease until I return. It is big enough for us to live and work."

"Ted would do anything to make your mother mad."

"I knew we could count on him."

Outside the fog lifted like a theater curtain and the sunlight coursed in a winter slant across the whole dining room, causing dozens of sparkles from the crystal table-glasses and chandeliers. The guests fell silent, everyone looking out at Green Park. The waiters made their way to the French windows, opening a few to clear out the cigarette smoke. Sims said it was an omen and put his hand over on Owen's, lingering a bit.

The trip to Winchester worked out, the two men arriving in the market town late on a Friday afternoon, walking from the train over to Old Vine Inn on Great Minster Street. The cathedral was just across the way.

"Two young lieutenants all the way from London. How lucky we are," the proprietress said, checking them in. There was an aroma in the inn, both tobacco and the oak firewood.

"May we go right to our room to freshen up?" Sims asked.

"Follow me."

Their room was up a narrow flight of dark-oak stairs, to a landing and up again. The floor upstairs slanted slightly towards the street, the door to the room already open.

It was paneled in the same dark oak as the stairs, heavy square beams close above their heads. A fire was lit in the fireplace, a single small lamp lit with a vermilion shade beside the four-poster bed. There would be no reading in bed. Prints of hunting dogs lined the walls.

"We just have the one bed, but it is large enough for two."

Sims was quick with a reply, "We're cousins from a family where everyone slept together, two or three to a bed. No problem at all."

"Splendid, then. Just ring the buzzer there for more firewood, or whatever you might require."

"We shall."

Sims and Owen were quick to take off their uniforms, folding them with care on the wall-side bench. It was warm in the room, comfortable enough to lie atop the bed without a coverlet. Owen was the first to start the movements into love, his hand caressing Sims's chest and arms. Then they turned towards one another, arms around each other. For a long few minutes they just held the other, savoring the joy of closeness and kissing. It had been a long year since the two men had been alone together, privately alone.

At seven o'clock the men redressed in their uniforms and walked downstairs to the public rooms, taking stools at the long bar for their first whisky and sodas.

"I've been thinking about our studio, after we get home," Sims said. "I have the first book all in my head, ready to write down. Even the title, which I will not share yet. It's about us, growing up, discovering each other, falling in love, learning to hide our feelings from the others, finding places we can be together, almost being discovered several times at university, going to the war, meeting at country inns like this one, and the rest. It will be a full account of our love story, the people who tried to stop us, the cousins who helped us, the uncle who knew everything, and how we came back from the army to start a new life. It won't take long because I know all the chapters, all the paragraphs. I'll put the finished manuscript in the safe deposit box at the bank and wait until it can be published. Then I will start to write the other stories I have in my head. These will take longer, stories that can be read by others without a hoopla."

"I know you will write great novels, Sims. Be a full success. I wonder about myself and the paintings I want to do. It is as if there were a glow from around the corner, I know something is afire there. I just need to learn how to turn the corner."

"Owen, you'll be an important painter, I know."

"I would like to be good rather than important. I don't have the first paintings fully formed in my mind, like you do your books, but I see the forms in the mist. Forms that excite me. We are so lucky to have each other."

"Do you think a painter and a writer can live their whole lives together, be in love until they are old and rickety?"

"I am sure of it. However, we should go west, Owen,

away from Philadelphia. Maybe all the way to the coast of California — Laguna or Carmel."

"And, on the very slight possibility that we are not the great painter and acclaimed writer we expect, we still have the life together."

The two men continued their talk over dinner, talk of a glorious new world they thought awaited them. These were secrets that most people kept to themselves, but the cousins had long learned the beauty of having a nearby sympathetic ear. They knew how rare it was, and particularly knew that in the war they had met so many men without it.

Prestor McCain had a small library in his adobe house about five hundred yards from Summerville House. From the catalog of an architectural remnants store in New York City, he had purchased a complete paneled room, probably once a waiting foyer for a more capacious French salon, but perfect for his purpose as a room to keep his books. Shelves were arrayed across one wall, the others offering a pair of windows, an entry door, a small fireplace, all interspersed with floor-to-ceiling bleached oak panels in robust carvings. The room included a similar bleached-oak parquet floor, not entirely level or in a single plane. In the waning days of the war, just to clinch the sale, the remnants store was happy to pay for shipping so far west. It was an odd space for the town of Santa Fe, New Mexico, but Prestor loved it all the more for that reason, closely overseeing its installation by local carpenters and craftsmen with a series of unwanted, running lectures on the excellence of French design. It had been finished for over a year now. McCain spent the morning hours in his French room, absorbing its quiddity, reading the new books that arrived every week in the post.

His work as a New York literary agent was officially over, but in this small room he kept up an active correspondence with authors, publishers, and other agents. If not in the center of the book world, he treasured his emeritus position, being a source of valuable opinions and considered recommendations for those who were still in the hurly-burly. He was assured that the Prestor McCain imprimatur still had clout in the city of publishers and writers. He imagined himself a Hadrian, retreated to the sylvan Tivoli, waiting for urgent requests for his wisdom from Rome.

His neighbor with the admirable name of Sims Summerville was a fledgling novelist, with several as yet unpublished manuscripts. McCain had finished reading the current one, what they referred to back in the city by the not-so-complimentary title of *An Experimental Novel*, and Sims was scheduled to arrive for a discussion in a few minutes. McCain wanted to organize comments in his mind, to clear a pathway through them from beginning to end. He would start with the compliments, picking a clause or phrase from here and there in Summerville's manuscript, to make the writer feel at ease. Then a detailing of the structure and how it was affecting the way the reader understood the story, good and bad. A talk then about the story itself, if it was worth the telling. And finally a list of faults and imperfections, going quickly over to how they might be remedied. How many times before had he done this? Many. And how often did it result in an admirable book? Not so many. Literary agents had to remember to call with silent condescension the work a "project," an embryo, not at all a "book" yet. There was a knock at the door.

"Come in and welcome, Sims," McCain said, motioning him to sit in one of the leather wing chairs facing each other by the fireplace. They talked for a while about the weather, the dinner party they had recently both attended, and other incidental matters. McCain had forgotten what a fine head of hair Sims Summerville had, good, widely spaced eyes and the tall, athletic stance of a tennis player or competitive swimmer. The book world in New York would appreciate these qualities, unliterary as they might be.

"Let's talk about your project. Please tell me what you had in mind."

"I had this image for a long time...a large shattered mirror in the basement of my family's house," Sims said. He was prepared to answer, as he had supposed McCain would ask a version of this, questioning the structure right from the beginning.

"The glass had not fallen out of the frame, but was splintered outwards around a circle, where I supposed someone had thrown a rock in anger. I knew then I wanted to write a book that way, to make chapters on each of the various splinters, going out like a nimbus or a spider web, reflecting different and not necessarily adjoining parts of the basement. It was all there, but rearranged. The impact circle gave a hint of violence, but well in the past, not of danger now."

"And why should this be a good pattern for a novel?"

"Well, I knew Tennyson used a 'mirror crack'd from side to side', so it might impart a gravitas for me. I think he saw himself apart from the world, and even further away in the broken mirror. I wanted to tell a story with some ambiguous parts, mysteries that eventually might be revealed. Some, not at all. I thought the shattered mirror did this. It showed pieces of the reflected room, but in an odd, disoriented order. Ceiling next to floor, door angled into cupboard. These variously shaped pieces gave me the chance to make chapters of different lengths, some only a page or two of reveries, others filled with many pages of dialogue. Only at the end is the whole picture revealed, and even then not entirely."

"You've obviously thought this out. So why is it better to tell in this scrambled way rather than a straightforward way?"

"At the beginning I thought it might be self-important, an oddness for its own sake. But as I wrote I realized it was a way to hear many different voices that a longitudinal, chronological story could not. It would be like evidence taken from a long list of witnesses, a patchwork of ideas, some moving the story along, others resting inactive in their circles of details."

"That's well said," McCain said, pouring out a cup of coffee for each of them from a thermos. He stood with his cup and walked to the window. He read aloud several examples of well-wrought sentences from Sims's manuscript. "Let me say, I admire your writing."

"Thank you, sir. Is there a 'but' after that?"

"But...I think the mirror structure needs work. It's confusing in places. I have marked those in red. I see you have written passages afterwards to join the disparate parts but the apartness seems too obvious. Like bandages poorly applied or crude wooden inserts holding an old piece of furniture together. I have marked those, too. They can be worked on. And I wonder which of your characters is the *true* narrator."

"I deliberately chose not to have a main narrator."

"I can see that. I just question the wisdom of it. You'll have to convince me more."

"I also thought that the shattered mirror was a good metaphor of what a man might see when he comes home from war. Not a cracked mirror, which could have happened passively, like a window left open on a frosty night or a maid mistakenly letting go of a broom handle. Shattered implies violence, somebody threw something. Much as the war itself."

"I like that reasoning, but let's have one of your characters be more equal among equals. It won't take much, but there should be some paragraphs early on to let us know, here is the wounded hero whose restorative adventures we will follow, the one who matters. And also on the backside of that coin, these are the others who matter, but not so much. Readers need clear road signs. The shattered idea gives your story more power, not something that happened just by accident."

"I see."

"If it were a matter of music, the cello is the surprise carrier of the theme, the rest of the string quartet uneasy, trying but not succeeding. Disharmony happens for a while, dissolving into harmony. Then, we are all happy to see that this fine fellow the cello will succeed."

"What do you think about my love story?"

"It is time for a man-loves-man story that does not end badly. We have had a number of those with Puritan punishments at the closing. I think your veteran of the European war status gives you rights of passage that other writers did not have, not exactly bullet-proof from the shots of ultra-Christian hand-guns, but nearly so. Love between men will startle those in some quarters, but you have to have lived behind the moon not to be aware of such love."

"Thank you, Mr. McCain. This has been most valuable."

"You are an able writer, Sims. Let's see what you do."

Sims shook the older man's hand and left the library.

How exciting, he thought, to be given a map forward, where to go. He knew that Prestor McCain was right in all he said, like the expert ear fine-tuning the score of a concerto. Not enough music here, too much there. He hustled across the garden and down the street, almost running back to his writing house. He knew how to make the changes in a few days. All now seemed possible, the clouds lifted to reveal a sunny horizon.

McCain did not wait to see the rewrite. His nose was twitching with ideas for this Sims Summerville, the aspiring novelist. Here was the first substantial anti-war novel since D-Day, with several provocative sexual themes, done to this young writer's odd but effective structure, a broken-by-a-thrown-rock mirror. The WASP circles of his Philadelphia and Main Line alone could purchase ten thousand copies, looking on each page for themselves in the chapters, with many more books bought to sit on high society tables all along the East Coast. Even the West Coast and Midwest could be in on this. London might soon be calling. He could almost write the jacket blurb in his mind, seeing the mirror image spilling across the cover. His favorite house for this one was Small and Redd. He knew the managing editor from years of after-work cocktails, talking about what it was that made a splendid book versus a mere popular work. This would be a worthwhile long-distance call to his private telephone number, which he found in a small book.

"Harry, you are going to love me, love me," he said without a hello.

"I already love you, Prestor. So what have you unearthed in the harsh red soil of New Mexico?"

"Wonderful things, Harry."

"We all thought you might be dead, your scalp drying on a juniper post."

"You'll see. Pay close attention to a simple parcel in brown wrapping paper from me in a couple of weeks."

"Not so much as a hint about what it contains?"

The telephone went dead with a click.

COAT AND TIE

M y god, three thousand hours," Hank said, reading a letter he had just opened. He and Owen were sitting on a bench in the plaza downtown, just coming from the post office where they retrieved the registered mail letter. They had been doing errands downtown.

"What about it?"

"That's the number of hours I will have to work a half-a-day for the judge before I can be certified as an attorney."

"Let's break it down," Owen answered. "Four hours a day, times five days a week. That's twenty hours, times fifty-two weeks is over a thousand hours. So it means just less than three years of work."

"*Only* three years. But, I guess that is about the same as three years actually going to Law School."

"Exactly."

"So Viona's uncle Octavio has agreed. I'll work four hours each morning as his clerk, a judge's clerk. Then I can help Gilbert in the station in the afternoon. I know he will be on board with that."

"A lot of hard work, hon. In the end, though, you'll be an attorney."

"I think that's what I want."

"It was your idea, so yes. Don't you know I love you just as much as a grease-monkey? Maybe even more. There was something alluring and compelling about the aroma of motor oil."

"I know it's what I should do. You and Sims have your silver spoons and your paintings and Sims's new book. The only way I can try to be on your level is to become a professional. I can't be a doctor or an architect, but in three years I could be Hank Garcia, Attorney-at-Law, welcome to my book-lined office."

"Think of it. Come to bed, Officer of the Court. You can wear your black robes while the three of us figure out how to make some new laws."

"I like the sound of it."

"And, by the way, you're on our level just as you are."

"I love you for saying it. So it all starts tomorrow. The footnote instructs that a coat-and-tie is a must at Judge Octavio Salazar's office on Palace Avenue. He's Viona's uncle, brother to her mother."

"So she was a Salazar. Rita's mother was a cousin to the Salazars, so that's how they are related."

"It's hard to follow, sometimes."

Owen said, "But let's go buy you some coats and ties. It will be my and Sims's gift to you, to celebrate."

"A black one and a brown one?"

"No, two black ones. He was a somber man, that lawyer, always in a severe black. It was said behind hands that he had many lovers who he turned to after a difficult hearing. His fine black garments strewn willy-nilly on the floor, joy on the sheets."

"I can't wait."

UNATTRACTIVE AND PLAIN

Isabel Summerville was planning a large, seasonal reception for her friends on the eighteenth of December, well earlier than other scheduled family get-togethers so as not to give anyone an excuse to decline. She had ordered holly wreaths with berries from an upstate farmer and long-needled pine ropes to festoon along the stair in the main entry. The girls in the kitchen were set to work making dozens of red-velvet bows to adorn the sconce lights and entry lamps. It would be the talk of season, she thought, like the old times.

She called her sister Augustine Parcher. "Dearie, meet me downtown for lunch. We can park at the bank and walk next door to the French restaurant."

"Good. I've been bored all morning. Just at twelve?"

"See you there."

Isabel had an errand she also wanted to do after lunch. The Christmas reception was an event when she could wear the long strand of matched pearls, the ones bought for her mother when her father was US Consul Fairfax in Shanghai fifty years ago, a position almost as important as the full ambassador in Peking. With time the large pearls came down to her and had become so valuable now that they lived in the family safe deposit box most of the time, brought out for occasions such as this gala reception. Augustine, in turn, had received the brooch with a circle of pigeon-blood red Burmese rubies their father bought at the same time, so there was no envy between the sisters, a sense of parity maintained.

After the two women ate about half of their chicken salad lunches made with peeled grapes, capers, and a cream vinaigrette, they went together to the bank where Borden Summerville maintained his office. They would not bother him, but go directly down to the safe deposit boxes. The clerk beside the circular gate recognized and welcomed them both. They had not brought their own keys, since Isabel was well aware of the owner's family privileges.

"Which drawer do you want, Mrs. Summerville? There are two for the family, you know."

"I forget, Mr. Brown. Please open both and we'll look."

The pearls were there in their case in the first drawer, but never ones not to slake their curiosity, the sisters decided to see what was in the other drawer. It held a stack of deeds, legal papers with blue enclosures, a heavy walnut box with Borden's collection of gold coins from around the world, and a manuscript with a blank cover.

Augustine picked it up. "Why this is your Sims's manuscript. The one he wrote at the Elm Street Studio. I'll just take it and read it."

"He was so standoffish about it that he put it in the safe deposit box."

"No matter. I'm a fast reader. Do you want to read it, too?"

"Perhaps. Let me know when you're done."

"Goody, goody."

At home Augustine placed the manuscript on the bedside table for reading in the evening, as she did every night with Isaac going to sleep quickly with eyeshades and ear-plugs, the lamp on his side of the bed turned off. This night Augustine's bedside light did not turn off until well into the early morning.

The Parchers arrived early for Isabel's party while the staff was lighting the candles and encouraging the fireplaces with an antique bellows. Augustine held onto her news about the manuscript for the moment, realizing that the better time for her disclosure would come later to more effect. After the holiday drinks had been passed and the long buffet table repeatedly attacked by the several dozens of guests, carols sung, coffee and pastries were served in the separate garden room facing out to the lighted evergreens in the far garden. Augustine felt the hours drag by in slow succession. Most of the guests took the hint from the first man announcing that he must take his wife home and with the hubbub of the retrieval of furs and coats, the party diminished into the still starry night with the lingering aroma of automobile exhaust in the driveway. Only the Parchers and the Summervilles remained, Borden mixing them all a final whisky and soda. They sat together by the fireplace.

"It all came together again, Isabel, a fine party," Augustine said, feeling unable to go much further with small talk and bringing up the matter foremost in her mind, "and I hate to bring up unpleasant news."

"Then don't," Borden said.

"But I must. I have finished Sims's still thankfully unpublished novel. We are all in it, in a thinly veiled narrative. Sims moved the action to Boston instead of Philadelphia, used other names, other businesses, but we are all so easily recognizable. Wicked boy. He even has the white streak in your hair, Isabel."

"That's to be expected," Isabel said. "Novelists always write about what they know, their own family and friends."

"The disagreeable part is that both Sims and Owen are revealed as homosexuals, cavorting about in the army in London with other men, and Sims portrays both their fathers as closeted homosexuals. Men hiding from their true nature by marrying a pair of rich, high-born sisters, so unattractive and plain that they had no hope of marriage otherwise."

"That clever boy managed to get an arrow through all our hearts in a single novel," Isaac said, smiling.

"Augustine, that's why it's called fiction," Borden said, standing up to poke the fire. "Novels are fiction. Besides, neither of you are unattractive and plain."

"But Sims just sold the *The Mirror Shattered* to Small and Redd."

"So?"

"Then, don't you think the wily publishers know about this earlier novel, a potboiler just waiting for the typesetters? Strike while the iron is hot."

"You are making too much out of it, my dear," Isaac said. "Remember, Sims was always the inventive one, telling us long stories and leading his cousins astray. Harmlessly astray, I might add."

"Well, I think we should just burn it," Augustine said.

"Nero burned all the scrolls and tablets that mocked his imperial self. That turned out well for him."

"You make mockery of it, Isaac, but I think this is a true family crisis. There are also lurid passages of men making love to one another. *Lurid*."

"Which kept you up well after midnight. It might well be Sims's first top of the bestseller list."

"Well, I intend to confront Sims about this, why he and Owen were lovers from so early on. In his very bedroom while we slept, in fact."

"You cannot," Isabel said, "just mention that we plucked his manuscript from the safe deposit box, mistaking it for a book of Quaker hymns."

"Exactly what do you expect to say, Augustine?" Borden asked. "There is nothing you can admit to without revealing your shared villainy. I think you should quietly return the pilfered manuscript to the safe deposit box tomorrow. No charges brought for the thieves. We'll forget about it."

"You all think this is so funny and inconsequential. Villainy, indeed. Just wait."

"After all, it was his private property, Augustine," Isabel said. "Perhaps he intended it to stay always in the lock box, like a private journal to be read after so many decades. But, I should also read it before we return it to the bank." She stood up to signal them all that this was the end of the evening and the matter.

But it would stay like tiers of clouds lurking way off on the horizon for all of them and especially the parts that were glossed over and not fully explored. Particularly those parts where both Borden and Isaac were not what they seemed? They had fathered children, after all. And, just how unattractive were the sisters? Why did their beloved, placid Sims write with such an acid pen? Would he, in fact, publish this work or burn it himself? Would he wait to publish when everybody involved was dead? What would the rest of their families think? Would the waiting clouds eventually come together into a literary storm? So many unknowns from her innocent reading of a nephew's book, Augustine thought. Warts on their noses, humbug.

ENGLISH VILLAGE LIFE

I t was Sims who insisted they all go to the performance, two Bach cantatas with a short intermission between them. They arrived early enough to get seats in the middle of Saint Francis auditorium, to hear the group of thirty-five English musicians, all men, on tour throughout the west. One the trumpeters was also a novelist and had written Sims from New York before their arrival. While he was in Santa Fe, Derek Stonewell wanted to meet the writer of *The Mirror Shattered* which, he wrote, had taken the London book world so much by storm. Please write back to their Boston agent, if that was possible.

Sims knew that although the book had sold well in England, there were many snide reviews about the American upstart. London was hard on its own writers and never open to letting a Yank squeeze into their world without some whipping, he was a new boy, after all. It was certainly not a storm of admiration, as Stonewell suggested. The trumpeter said he was so delighted to be seeing America and to be out of the grim days of English rationing and lack of winter heat. He responded quickly to Sims's invitation to have the whole orchestra and chorus to a late-night supper at Summerville House after the concert. *You Yanks are so generous.*

Sims, Owen, and Hank would lead the way back to the house, six other cars hired to carry them all, even if it required a number of them to sit on top of one another. Rita was setting up a buffet dinner and Perfecto was chilling the wine, lighting the fires. Rita's trusty cousins in black trousers and white shirts were on the standby, a big party like the old times for Summerville House when the ladies ruled the roost.

At the auditorium, the first selection was *Cantata 191 Gloria in Excelsis Deo* and Sims saw the man he was sure was Derek Stonewell in the row of four trumpets, just in front of the chorus. He saw the tortured look, unruly hair of a young English novelist. The trumpets, horns, recorders, violins, tympani, and chorus started at full tilt right from the beginning, revealing the glorious joy that Bach brought every Sunday to Leipzig.

The conductor, named Julian Barth, an elegantly thin man, made graceful swoops with the baton in his right hand as his left palm rose high with fingers outstretched, then descended to turn over a page, a curvaceous sort of metronome. Sims reached for Owen's hand as the music continued, remembering that they had heard this at Saint Martin-in-the-Fields during the war, young lieutenants enjoying the first joys of Europe, enduring the war with grace. It was also the first night they had to make love together in London, Owen finding them a small room he knew in a back street of St. James. Sims reached on the other side for Hank's hand, bringing a surprised, but pleased look from Hank.

The English streamed out of the cars in groups of three and four, leaving their cased instruments with one of Rita's cousins on the front portal, and went happily into the brightly lit Summerville House, candles on every flat surface. The dining table was filled with plates, a buffet of carved ham, carved roast beef, loaves of bread with butter, dishes with tamales, vegetables, corn pudding, enchiladas, cheese souf-flés, and a whole range of frosted desserts. Rationing and shortages were still the norm back in England, and this was a gastronomical explosion for the men.

"So, Sims," said Derek, "when I wrote you some weeks ago I never expected this bounty. Thanks so very much, indeed. You don't know how precious food is until you haven't had it for a decade."

"Rita is our treasure. We are happy to share her."

"I read your book and found it fascinating," Derek said. "What are you working on now?"

"A different sort of story, but another man trying to make sense of the war."

"A theme that never seems to grow old."

Sims wondered if that was a compliment or heavily cloaked dig. He remembered the sharp tongues of London, saying one thing and meaning another. Since he was the host, with ingrained family instructions on the necessary goodness of a host, he would keep his mouth shut on the matter.

"What about your work?" Sims said. "What are you writing now?"

"Light tales of English village life in the thirties, before the war."

"Very popular books, I understand."

"Happily so. It is a series, so I can keep it going for a lifetime."

"A good life."

"It seems better here, though. The three of you in such a love-nest."

Sims had not realized that the true nature of their three-some was so transparent. But he remembered that the English were quick to smell a scent of oddness, and they relished in finding it. Bold questions in the war were the norm with young British aides-de-camp in London headquarters, the Americans slow to answer.

"We were lucky to find one another."

"How does it work exactly? Who's on top?"

"We take turns, Derek. Excuse me now."

He found Hank being talked to by the tall conductor, who at the concert he decided was one of the seven or eight homosexuals of the ensemble. Sims knew that Hank could not handle himself well when men came on to him, so he better go to the rescue.

"Oh, Sims, glad you are here," Hank said. "Julian was telling me about a military bar in Soho. Very odd things going on there."

"Not so very odd by my reckoning," Julian said, trying to cut up the roast beef on his plate with a fork. "You lot would love it."

"I well remember Soho from my time in London," Sims said, "since American second-lieutenants were prohibited from going, we couldn't wait."

"There you are, then. Groups from all over making love together."

Sims wondered if their threesome relationship had been the exhaustive topic of conversation on the long bus trip across the plains to Santa Fe. Had Derek expounded on the rich American queers they were going to meet, and how very more queer it was that there were three of them together? It had begun to be annoying. Hank seemed to not be aware of the perfidy going on.

The evening continued with many other discourteous remarks from the English group, gathering around the piano to sing the familiar-to-them refrain of *Nymphs and Shepherds, Jolly Good.* The only good thing the ensemble did was to end the evening early since they had to depart for Denver at dawn the next morning. They piled back into the hired cars and it was finally quiet again at Summerville House. The three hosts fell onto the leather sofa.

"Wow," Owen said. "Was that a mistake, or what? I haven't been grabbed that way since boarding school."

"I had two offers of blow-jobs out in the garden," Hank said.

"I apologize," Sims said. "Who would think? I suppose tomorrow we'll hear stories of what they asked Rita's cousins to do."

"All those Englishmen seemed to think we were having a full-time orgy here," Hank said.

"One man told me that he had heard Santa Fe was like Capri in the twenties," Owen said. "They were so sorry they did not have the time to stay a while and join in."

"The English are supposed to be polite and elegant. It's true — no good deed goes unpunished," Sims said.

FINDING PARADISE

Alberta had not absorbed the misty landscape or the lemon-tree warmth of the South of France into her paintings, but instead pulled from her imagination the many pueblo dances she and Malvina had attended over the years in New Mexico. Not entirely realistic, the canvases depicted long rows of dancers coiling this way and that, with midsummer storms looming above. Her colors were earthen — ochres, sienna reds, pale sky blues, corn yellows, deep umbers, burnt blacks. Paris, as always in love with the idea of the American West, fell deeply for her pictures of the first peoples, so unlike the refined denizens of civilized France.

Some of her canvases had the top three-quarters devoted to the storm clouds, rain about to inundate and overpower the small pueblo plazas below, curving lines of dancers encircling the square buildings. Dust came up in small spirals, everything below appearing to be dry with the rain-heavy storm about to flood the land. Each canvas told a different story, but all with the same theme of harsh nature surrounding the first ideas of civilized life, native peoples at risk of horrid, punishing natural events.

She had come to her opening night in a finely pleated, maroon silk dress from an Italian designer and a necklace of chunky garnets, perhaps hoping for the look of a Maltese priestess taken out of her element for just one evening. Eschewing her usual attire of men's trousers, Malvina wore one of her rare attempts at a long dress, a severe black affair done up by a Menton seamstress, and she added an oversized brooch of silver circles. Artistic Paris was entranced by the pair of offbeat ladies, perhaps hearing echoes of Gertrude Stein and Alice B. Toklas, another product of Sapphic America.

There was a painting on an easel in the front window of the Galerie de Foche, an enterprise of Martine de Foche and her brother, Igor, a not-so silent partner. Martine was a small, dark-haired woman, teetering on very high heels, and Igor was tall and dark. Alberta thought Igor moved about the opening night crowd in languorous curves like the man in the Toulouse-Lautrec posters, Valentin the Boneless. He only lacked the tall black hat. The evening was one of the siblings' first gallery exhibits since the war and Alberta, on their recommendation, was going by only her first name. Sister and brother were trying very hard to exude the spirit of modernity. The outside banner, hanging sideways beside the front door, said in block letters *ALBERTA!!!*

Several of the paintings had been sold before the four young people from Santa Fe came in, excited to be included in the middle of metropolitan art. They had arrived a few days before, after a train ride to New York, a steamship crossing, Le Havre, the train to Paris, and finally a taxi to rooms reserved at the Hotel des Sts. Peres, where Malvina and Alberta were staying and had suggested they also stay. Malvina's invitation a couple of months earlier included a generous check to pay for the whole trip and detailed instructions for their every move along the way. Avoiding any of the clan her own age in Philadelphia, Malvina asked for the support of her younger New Mexico family, who should drop everything and attend, which they dutifully did.

Owen, Sims, Hank, and Viona caught the eyes of the gallery first-nighters, attractive young Americans always a succulent meal. Igor de Foche, in particular, almost salivated, eyes on stalks, as they came through the front door, immediately recognizing who they were and how they were related to the painter Alberta. With a nod to the men, he took Viona by the arm and with sweeping gestures introduced her around the gallery. Left on their own, Owen, Sims, and Hank took glasses of the champagne being passed and walked slowly around, looking at the paintings. Beside one of the canvases, they came upon Alberta, by chance alone.

Hank was the first to speak. "I very much like the paintings. You've captured what I feel is New Mexico."

"I did not expect these," Owen said. "They have an expert and subtle power."

"Thank you, boys, but I think Martine and Igor are vastly disappointed."

"How could they be?"

"They somehow thought I was a real Pueblo maiden when I sent the paintings. They imagined I would attend in beaded moccasins and turquoise beads with a large braid down my back. Oddly provincial of them, don't you think?"

"From the sold markers, I think they may be getting over it."

"Just so. And, Owen, I want to hear about your work when we all go back to Menton. We'll talk there."

Igor deposited Viona upon a circle of French people and quick-stepped his way to where the men and Alberta were standing. Sims had thought from the outset that his taking Viona around was a ruse, because he saw a roguish, other-side-of-the-fence look. Igor now made that supposition right.

"Three attractive young men. We are so very f-f-fortunate."

"You have a wonderful gallery here," Sims said. "Are you a painter, Igor?"

"No, no. Just *le propritaire*. My sister was the painter in her girlhood."

"Do you show her work here?"

"No, she gave it up to be the gallery owner."

"You might also consider Owen's work for exhibit. Owen Parcher here."

"I shall. And are you an artist as well?"

"No. I write novels."

"And what does your d-d-dark-haired friend do?"

Here it was, Sims thought, the real focus of Igor's lust was Hank. Igor had been circling around his chosen quest, waiting to attack when the herd was divided, distracted, defenses down. It was the carnivore picking out the most vulnerable, now toying with his prey.

"Tell Igor what you do, Hank."

"I hope to be a lawyer, but right now I am a greasemonkey."

"*Mais oui,* I actually know what a g-g-greasemonkey is. You repair automobiles."

"Good for you," Sims said. "And, Igor, Hank is also our beloved, innocent friend, and we are very protective of him."

"I see his innocent eyes, but there is no need to protect. I can understand why he is beloved. Let me and Martine take all of you to dinner tonight when the exhibit is over. In about an hour at the restaurant around the corner, *Roger le*

Grenouille. Hank and I can t-t-talk about the law, automobiles, and their repair."

Alberta, amused at the sensual swirls her young friends had mustered, said, "We will meet you there at nine, Igor. Very generous to take us all out. A table for eight, I think."

As they waited for the exhibit to be over, circulating around the gallery and pausing in front of each painting in turn, Sims said to Hank, "Be prepared, friend and lover, for an all-out, D-Day assault from our stuttering friend, Igor."

"Should I just go back to the hotel and wait?"

"No. You can handle yourself. Take it as a compliment."

"It is somehow good to be noticed."

"I would think in advance about what to do with his wandering hands at dinner. Maybe it's not a great idea for your f-f-famous, left-handed cold-cock."

"I won't, but I wish he wanted you or Owen. Either of you would know what to do."

At the restaurant, there was no way the host Igor would not sit next to Hank, with the others parceled out around the circular table. From Sims's viewpoint, the dinner seemed to go without incident, he keeping a sharp eye on his at-risk friend. Igor was an able impresario, keeping the table conversation going but taking the moments when others were talking to speak with hushed tones to Hank. It was an impressive performance, going from a raconteur's on-stage announcements to *sotto voce* off-stage with ease, back and forth at a moment's notice. Hank appeared to be enjoying himself, nodding, smiling, and on one occasion even putting his hand over on Igor's arm. Sims worried that Hank was leading the man along.

At the hotel, Hank said, "He's an interesting guy."

"I'll bet," Owen said.

"No, really. I know he wants to get into my pants, but he was a gentleman."

"How so? He looked like a hungry wolf to the rest of us."

"Did you know he is a Buddhist? Studied in Indochina. Wants to open a study center here in France so people can come learn about Buddhism."

"Especially for supple young men?"

"Okay. Okay. He's a dirty old man. But I like him."

"Take care, sweetheart. I think we've opened the lid of your rosewood box a bit too far. I can smell the distinct odor of m-m-m-musk."

The next day Owen wanted to take the others to the Cezanne exhibit in the upstairs rooms of the Jeu de Paume. They walked around the center of Paris afterwards, having lunch at a small bistro with outdoor tables, Sims ordering for all of them *l'omelette aux fines herbes* and a green salad. Several carafes of wine later, they walked back across the river to their hotel. A full tour of Paris would have to wait for another trip.

Early the next morning, Malvina, Alberta, and the four from Santa Fe took the train south and over along the coast to Menton. It was to be a relaxed two weeks for visiting, meeting the women's friends on the Cote-d'Azur, getting to know one another. Malvina had already rented chairs for them on the beach in front of the old hotel, as well as an open account at the adjoining bar down the path through an overgrown, semi-tropical garden. Guy Martel met the train with the Hispano-Suizza for the ladies and he had hired a man with a car large enough to hold everybody else and the luggage. There were bedrooms for them in the old stone house, for Viona and Hank in single beds in separate rooms, with a wardrobe and a chair in each. Owen and Sims were given a double bed in their own room. The bathroom was down the hall for everybody. Clearly, Malvina and Alberta had discussed exact relationships and decided upon them, if incorrectly.

Malvina and Alberta stayed in their master suite at the far end downstairs, suitably away from their guests. Each upstairs guest window gave out on the citrus terraces, now redolent in bloom, the aroma of orange blossoms circulating through the house. Owen thought to himself that the two women had a nose for finding paradise, first Santa Fe and now Menton. He wondered if he would continue to follow their lead. How was it possible to move his now extended household, those dependent upon him, to Europe? It amused him to realize that he considered himself the father figure for his small group, a shepherd for his lambs. How had that come to be?

All of them fell into relaxed daily patterns in the southern warmth. Guy drove the four of them every day to the beach, retrieving them by mid-afternoon. It was a sandy beach, light ochre in color, with clear, shallow water out for several dozen yards. Hank and Viona had never been to a beach before, so the others taught them the first basics of swimming, holding their undersides while they learned to kick and float. Viona was a quick study, wanting to swim out in the deeper water after the first week. Hank was more reticent, so Owen spent more time with him, enjoying their closeness in the water.

After the tutorials, Sims, a strong swimmer, went way out each day, sometimes coursing around the headland out of sight, walking back on the coastal path. By the start of the second week, all of their sunburns had turned to tan and they talked about their sense of well-being, happiness.

As the visit was nearing its end, Malvina asked Owen to sit on the bench beside her in the garden. "I will miss all of you when you are gone."

"Thanks so much for making this happen."

"It was our pleasure. Alberta thought it was like having a small, well-meaning army on her side at the opening."

"We love Summerville House, and you are making another safe harbor here."

"I had thought when you arrived there that it was only you and Sims. Cousins in love."

"That's true."

"But I see your life has become more complex than that. Hank completes it handsomely."

"We feel lucky to have found each other."

"I know there will be people who disapprove. Alberta and I faced that in Santa Fe."

"I suspected so."

"Love must be so very rare in this world that people can be strongly envious when they see it in full bloom. They then disapprove."

"I know that."

"And I want to put it into words. As I watched the three of you at dinner the other night, the way you looked at each other, I knew it was right. I approve of the three of you heartily. And if it ever gets too difficult in Santa Fe, we can find you a place here. France is old-fashioned in other ways, but not in the world of love."

"I've come to the same conclusion."

"Just send me a note and I'll start looking."

"I've been daydreaming of moving us all to France."

"Keep it in your mind, then."

DON'T LINGER IN HANDKERCHIEFS

Owen and Viona were sitting at Rita's kitchen table having coffee while she prepared the food for dinner at the kitchen counter. It was a planned get-together, not a secret one but also not publicized among the other denizens of and visitors to Summerville House. Viona had a stack of official-looking documents in front of her.

"Do both of you really think it will work?"

"You're the perfect one," Rita said. "Your mother and your aunts were the only ones allowed to make the vestments for the cathedral for so many years, and you learned it all from them."

"I have made fifty or more dresses for myself and others in the Maes family over time, getting better and better. I have a feeling about it. A good one."

"We do, too," Owen said. "I just sold a painting for five hundred dollars and Rita has saved that amount at the federal bank. We are your silent partners."

"How did you save that much, Rita?" Viona asked.

"We spend only Perfecto's pay for our living expenses. I have kept all of mine in the federal savings bank. It has been our arrangement for a long time, even in the earlier years with Miss Summerville. A woman needs her own money."

"A thousand dollars sounds like a lot, but it will go

quickly," Owen said. "Your rent for the shop at La Fonda will be the most, supplies and store fixtures next, and if you have some salespeople, they will have to be paid by the week."

"For the first year, it will be just me in the shop."

"I can spell you on my day off," Rita said.

"My father, blessed saint that he is," Viona said, "made a plan with all the expenses laid out on a ledger. I will have to sell ten thirty-dollar dresses a month for the first year, twenty in the second year. My aunts are all ready to go, and I have the patterns cut out. I ordered the fabrics and supplies with my own money. We will have more than thirty plus dresses by the time we open. We've agreed to pay the aunts at the end of each year, to make ends meet and keep our cash on hand. They will be paid so much for each dress."

"You know, I come by the clothing business honestly," Owen said.

"How is that?" Rita asked, filling Owen's coffee cup.

"I worked in a men's haberdashery in college, Hofmeister's Haberdashery. Marvin Hofmeister was the owner and he inspected our outfits each day, lined up like the army. He wanted us in white button-down shirts, a diagonal stripe tie in solid colors, a good sport jacket, flannel slacks, and cordovan shoes. He told us before the doors opened, *Don't linger in handkerchiefs, boys, get the customer right over to the suits.* Suits were where the money was."

That was the first official business meeting of the three owners of Casa Viona, a ladies' fashion shop with windowed rooms beside the front entrance of La Fonda hotel, on the plaza. The longtime gift shop had just given up its lease, and Viona, Rita and Owen moved quickly to rent it and agreed to stay mum about their exact ownership.

Viona's extended family had several trained seamstress-
es, well accustomed to the fine points of high-end ladies'
dresses, not exactly haut-couture but several levels above
what was available at the downtown department stores.
Tanta Euclavia, the eldest of the unmarried aunts, had before the war worked in a fashion firm in St. Louis whose
head of production was a sharp-eyed Frenchwoman, teaching all the young girls secrets that were only known in Paris at the time...curved seams, ruched sleeves, and pleated
skirts. Euclavia had attended the Ursuline Academy after
she finished her studies at the Loretto Girl's School in town,
but she stayed on in St. Louis for several years, working at
the fashion shop, learning how to sew high fashion. She in
turn taught her sisters back in Santa Fe during the Depression years, the sisters applying their expertise to the vestments and chasubles of the clerics in Santa Fe churches and
garments for the townspeople. It was a valuable source of
income in down times. Visitors remarked on the excellence
of vestments and altar cloths so far from Rome, perhaps not
understanding why.

Casa Viona would do custom fittings and exclusive designs for an added price, but there would be many dresses
ready to buy in popular sizes. Viona hoped that it was an
idea which had been waiting for its time. In town, people
often came up to her, remarking on what it was she was
wearing, where it came from. She was sure that the women
of Santa Fe were hungry for her well-designed fashions.

Viona brought to the table what all the nimble-fingered
aunts could not, her splendid, original sense of style, an
ability that had to be innate, in the bone. From those dinner parties at Summerville House, both Rita and Owen noticed with admiration Viona's choices for evening wear, and

Owen was amazed to discover that she had sewn them all herself. The aunts taught her the technical parts of French sewing, but she surpassed her teachers early on, designing garments with a contemporary edge. The aunts were very proud of their Viona, a niece who encompassed their own secret hopes and desires.

The opening was set for a month ahead. Rita would cater from the kitchen at the house, Owen, Hank, and Sims serving as hosts and waiters. The Maes family carpenters made the cabinets, racks, and shelves. Viona designed the mannequins, all to match her slim frame. The sign painter for the church wrote the name in an elegant cursive on the windows. Ads were run in the New Mexican newspaper and written invitations went out to every important woman in town.

Thirty dollars was a great deal of money for a woman's dress in 1948, but there were other items as well. Women's slacks cost less, silk blouses also, as well as capes and scarves. All of them were designed by Viona. The only items she had to buy wholesale were the French women's espadrilles in a rainbow of colors, shipped by slow boat from Paris.

Everything else was designed and created by the Maes women: handkerchiefs, knit gloves, capelets, shorts, purses, and separate collars, each with a sewn-in black tag with white letters. There was an excitement and laughter at the family sewing machines, which could be heard stitching into the night hours in the adjoining Maes houses.

Mona Ellis sought Viona out at the opening. "My dear, I've admired your style since those dinners at Sims and Owen's house. Please help me pick something."

"I have a dress in a sky-blue over here you would like, I am sure."

"I guess it's right to match the eyes."

"Yes. I'll place it aside and you can come by later this week to try it on."

"I also like that black-and-white pattern."

"That, also."

Mona and her friends put away twenty dresses on the opening night, surpassing the whole month quota. In time, Rita's sisters and friends made their way to the shop, and it pleased Viona to give them an unspoken deep discount on dresses that were formerly priced at a week's salary, a secret kept by both sides. As several strata of Santa Fe's female community found happiness on the racks of Casa Viona, it gave hope that the shop would be around a while.

For Texas women in the postwar years, Santa Fe became their nearby version of what Paris was for English women — a place to spend a long weekend, shop, dine, imbibe, and admire the other strangers. The fine location at the entrance to Santa Fe's most prominent hotel ensured that tourists would see something new in this odd city. Women from Amarillo, Dallas, and Houston were quick to see the wisdom of combining a family holiday outing with pursuits of their own, boxed dresses sent quietly back by parcel post.

WAVING HIS ARMS ABOUT

Owen sat on the chair across from the easel, studying a canvas he had been working on for the last week. It was not going well, definitely not thriving. In fact, his whole career as a painter appeared to have stalled in shallow water. Sims was racing forward in his writing, his third novel being typeset in New York with a planned publishing date the first of October, a slot reserved for books with the highest expectations at Small and Redd. Hank had become the attorney for his mother's pueblo, San Ildefonso, as well as the farther north tribe of Mescalero Apaches, whose oil interests were starting to bring needed income. The pueblo and tribe both needed legal advice and felt safe with a lawyer connected by family to the pueblos, who even could speak a native language.

Owen knew he was not in competition with his lovers, but it would make life easier at Summerville House if he could claim a sold-out exhibit sometime or reviewers who saw enough promise to write about. The others sensed Owen was not keeping up with them, but did not know how to help him with a boost up. They had talked last night at dinner about the importance of equality, all three of them eye-to-eye.

As they lingered over coffee, Hank started the topic

with, "Don't you both think it is important for us all to be standing on the same step? In the beginning, I felt you both were way above me. But the law degree and starting the practice has caught me up."

"Owen and I never thought you were on a lower step than us," Sims said. "I am very glad that you feel on a level now."

"Me, too," Owen said. "If anything, it is me that was not keeping up. You both leaped ahead in your work, but painting has stayed still for me."

"Why do you think that is?" Sims asked.

"I had been hoping for a break-through. Some motif or idea that told me to go ahead, make it mine. I've read that Matisse said that a break-through was a clearing in the woods, the close-spaced trees no longer pressing up against you."

"Don't you think that the close-spaced trees will end? In their own time?"

"I get impatient, I know. I have dreams about big paintings that I cannot seem to get going. Maybe I should just start one, and if that one doesn't work, do another, and another. Right now there is a stack of large white canvases, leering back at me."

"Can we help?"

"Just talking about it makes it seem more possible."

Owen passed all these ideas over in his mind as he waited for sleep and wondered if there was a secret, large door through which the great painters passed, going into the hidden garden of art beyond, where all the secrets grew like perennials in an herbaceous border. Where was that door? And at what time of day was the lock going to be unlocked, the clicking sound to wonderful things beyond?

The next morning, he enrolled himself in a life drawing class, the classic tutorial for beginning painters of all sorts. He would start again. The class met twice a week at two in the afternoon at Parthon Ellis's capacious studio for two hours of uninstructed drawing. Parthon's painting, done so long ago, of Viona, in the slacks and black shirt she was wearing that first night, was still hanging on a side wall. She was leaning against the side of a doorway, a voluptuous curve. Owen thought for a moment about how long-lived a desire could be, how it lingered on in the mind. Poor Parthon.

The models were an assortment of local men and women, most of them easy without their clothes in front of a class. There were eight artists in attendance, including Parthon Ellis himself. His studio had a sixteen-foot ceiling and was forty feet long, a studio window across the entire north end. Attendees brought their own easels, supplies, and stools.

"Welcome, Owen," Parthon said. "I am pleased you decided to come, even though I know your work is non-objective and abstract."

"Every artist needs to draw."

"Indeed, and even I, after sixty years, learn something at every class."

Owen had come to like Parthon and go beyond his crusty, stuffy exterior. Even if he could not shed his East Coast image, he was a true artist, committed to helping the young make it in a difficult endeavor. There were definitely two Parthons — the eager-to-help artistic comrade in arms and the self-satisfied patriarch of tradition. The helpful one was the one in attendance in his studio this day. The one in whom desire lingered.

For this first day of the class for Owen there was a male nude, a well-built, early middle-age man named Oliver

Darge with large anchor tattoos on both arms and admirable muscles in his stout legs. He was a heavy-framed working man, the type the nineteenth century artists pictured pulling a rope, swinging a sledge hammer, or lifting an anvil in a leather apron, the red fires of a forge in the background. Owen used the customary charcoal stick on the newsprint pad, smudging here and there for shading. He concentrated on Oliver's legs, which seemed to him the most difficult parts to draw.

Oliver changed poses every ten minutes, sometimes stretching out his legs and at other times sitting with feet on the rungs of the stool. Owen's drawings went only slightly above the waist each time. By the second hour, he sensed a delight in his ability to catch the human form. Perhaps this was the something that he was waiting for. Parthon announced to the gathering that Oliver was between jobs, looking for a permanent place as a studio assistant. Did anybody know of a studio where he could work?

Owen wondered how he could use a studio assistant, as he preferred to be alone while painting, but he had heard of painters who had assistants to stretch the canvas, some even painting the first coat of color all over the canvas. Was that something that would work for him? That might just be the something new he needed, letting an assistant prepare the painting, giving him a boost up, making him think what to do with the deep orange color the assistant painted all over the canvas. Maybe it was worthy of a try, since so far his efforts were going nowhere.

"Oliver," he said as the class was leaving with their folded easels and stools. "Would you like to try working with me for a week or so? I have some ideas. Let's say a two-week tryout, to see how it goes."

"Fine, Owen. Do you want me to pose?"

"No, I'm an abstractionist. But I think you can help me."

"Intriguing. Sure, I'll give it a two-week try."

"So let's start tomorrow at nine. It's just across the road from Parthon's studio, over there." He pointed over there.

"What would the pay be?"

"Let's say thirty dollars for a five-day week, nine-to-four with one of Rita's lunches provided."

"What should I wear?"

"Dungarees, or something that can stand some dripped paint."

"Even more intriguing. See you tomorrow."

Only after he had made all the arrangements did he start to consider what Sims and Hank would think about a new male, a nude male, in their midst. They would both know that Oliver was not the type that Owen had ever been interested in sexually. He would bring up the subject casually at dinner, try to make it the same as if he was hiring another person to rake the lawns or stack the firewood. Both Sims and Hank were sensible sorts, not ever showing a glimmer of jealousy or suspicion. But perhaps there had been no reason for suspicion until now. He must try to walk lightly on this new road.

He was up early before Oliver was scheduled to arrive, looking at his recent canvases. There was a monastic, still quality to them, he thought, and they were good if a bit bloodless, antiseptic. Ouch. The drawings on newsprint of Oliver's legs were pinned up on his work board. What if he cropped sections of these drawings, losing any sense of their being legs, but focusing on the sinewy patterns of the muscles? He hunted for scissors and found them, cutting out square parts of the full drawings. It might just be possible to take these as a starting point, expand them to the large canvas size he wanted to work on. He cut out another square, and another. There was definitely a series here, sinuous lines that suggested male muscles, but still totally non-objective.

"Hello, are you ready for me?" Oliver said, walking in without knocking.

"I was just changing directions. I think I want you to model for me after all. I have an idea about using your legs as a place to begin a large, non-objective canvas."

"Wow. I remember you just drew my legs."

"Let's set you up over here and I can sketch the design right on the canvas."

"So I didn't need my dungarees, after all?"

"Sorry, are you okay with this?"

"It's fine. I've spent many hours modeling at Parthon's."

Oliver sat on the stool while Owen sketched in charcoal the long lines on a six-foot by six-foot canvas. Owen thought to repeat the leg sections again and again across the canvas, the same one repeated, making a frieze of sorts. Then he erased sections of that, as it seemed too formal, and interposed a larger drawing of a different part of Oliver's legs. He could see an elongated knee and top of the lower leg. He kept repeating the motif, each section a different scale, some no more than a curving line from top to bottom, others a circulating bit of business between the lines. More erasings and more additions and the cartoon for the first canvas was there. He knew better than to worry with small details at this stage. They all could be in-filled later, but it was important to keep the excitement of this first discovering going.

He heard in his mind the old art professor saying *Get right to the heart of the matter at the easel. Don't fuss.* So he mixed quickly some black oil paint with a white to make a deep gray, thinning it with turpentine, and with a large brush, using his charcoal lines as a pattern, painting in the basic, but complex composition in a single hour. He knew it would take several days to fill in with thicker, stronger colors.

The appearance of muscles was there, but not recognizable as Oliver's legs. There was an unquestioned feeling of masculinity, but reduced to graphic abstraction. How could mere lines delineate such strong maleness? This was the breakthrough he had been searching for. In a side of his mind, he thought ahead to other versions of the same motif, lines going in different directions, more detail across the middle, repetitions going sideways but in this first try the Goddess of Art had come down from her throne in the clouds to award him a winsome, first smile.

"Owen, you are great. In such a short time," Oliver said, looking at the canvas on his first break.

"If it goes quickly, it is usually right. I'll take a break, too."

"Where did you learn to do this?"

"I don't know, Oliver. There was a good professor, long ago, but really you just come that way or you don't."

"Like blue eyes. I've always wanted blue eyes like yours."

"Most people want brown, like yours."

They had forty-five minutes before lunch at the main house, so Owen followed another of his professor's dictums of getting the first layer of paint on quickly. He filled in the areas between the lines with either dark, warm black, which he mixed from Burnt Umber and Ultramarine, or a light, cool gray, from Raw Umber, Titanium White, and Cobalt Blue. The long bands of the muscles he overlaid with thin parallel lines, which curved and turned with the human form, like so many undulating guitar strings. There were drips going down across the canvas. He would have to decide how many of them to leave, that sense of moment a good part of the composition. The First Covering, as the teacher called it back in the school days, was done, a strong first step to a finished canvas.

Mr. Holdings-Brown was that professor, an excitable, high-voiced bachelor who could not resist jumping about as he talked, waving his hands about to make a point, his enthusiasm carrying over to even the lesser students. It was a Junior Year course and had the imposing title of Solving Problems of the Big Canvas. Owen could hear Holdings-Brown cooing approval over what had happened this morning. An idea formulated, the way forward thought about, then quick action to keep the idea alive, the hand executing the idea without quavering, no resistance to the grand sweeping gesture or GSG (very important in a Big Canvas), and stopping before the voices of fussiness took over. Then, still very important, you must step away and think. Owen was sure Holdings-Brown was happy, wherever he was, waving his arms about and saying *Step away, Owen.*

"Oliver, let's step away and have lunch."

NINETY-FIVE WORDS A MINUTE

S ims was taking a late-morning break from his writing schedule in the kitchen, having a cup of coffee and one of Rita's omnipresent ginger cookies. After three hours of writing, he had learned to give his hand a rest, some time off. He wrote the first draft of his novels longhand, editing as he went along, a yellow legal tablet, the pages with cross-outs and arrows bringing a later paragraph up to earlier in the story. The fountain pen he used was a gift from his mother, sent to him during his Army days in London. It was a Swiss-made, top-of-the-line black pen, larger than most other pens, black with a white circle around the top. It felt good in his hand right from the start.

The ink flowed easily from the wide nib and he enjoyed the process of writing even though his left-handedness made him angle the paper up so he did not smudge the newly written ink. He kept the first draft in a three-ring notebook, using a punch device to puncture the holes on each page. At the end of each day of writing, he estimated the number of words written and wrote the number off to the right of the page. Along with the date and the total for the project. *2300 words - 6 July 1947 - 29,210 words.* Perhaps it was an odd form of vanity and hubris to keep track this way, but it pleased him the next morning to see what was and what might be done.

When he completed the first draft, it was time for the typewriter. Not a bad typist, Sims was capable during his army years of ninety words a minute with no mistakes. His services as an editor then were sought after by the higher-ups, giving him more than the usual number of three-day passes. He had slowed down since the army but could type out all of a first draft in several days. He also placed that typescript into a three-ring folder the same way as the hand-written one. Like bread dough, the writing needed time to rise on its own before the oven. Often that was a week or so before Sims started to work with a red pencil, wearing an editor's hat, closing in on inconsistencies, awkward parts, repeated words, and redundancies.

Rita came in as he was finishing the coffee.

"Good morning, Mr. Sims. How is it going?"

"Well, thanks, Rita. Letting my hand rest for a spell."

"I have a young cousin, Jason, who could help you."

Sims resisted a smile, because they had at dinner just recently discussed that Rita had a cousin to solve almost everything. There was a seamstress to make new sheets for the odd-sized beds at Summerville, a tall young cousin to clean the windows, a short one to fix the plumbing under the kitchen counter, a cousin who could bring fresh eggs every week, a cousin to bring firewood, apple cider, spicy sausages, piñon nuts, or the comely ones to wait at table on party nights. The extended Sanchez family seemed able to solve any and all of the missing pieces of the civilized life, a small fee for each resolution.

"How is it that Jason can help?"

"He has just finished the course to become a court secretary. Types ninety-five words a minute, no mistakes."

"I can see how he can help. Would he be able to read my handwriting?"

"Sí, Mr. Sims. There are too many court reporters now, so he is looking for something until a court job opens up."

"Please ask him to come by tomorrow at nine, Rita. I have a new manuscript almost ready."

"He has his own typewriter with a carrying case. A Smith-Corona with black-and-red ribbon the family bought for his graduation."

"I can promise that we won't wear out the red part of his ribbon."

The word was sent through the Sanchez family communication system and Jason was hired to type Sims's manuscripts. By coincidence he would start the same day as Owen's new studio assistant, Oliver. Quiet days at Summerville House might be coming to an end.

Jason arrived right on time at nine o'clock the next day. Sims saw the Sanchez family resemblance in the young man, the long Spanish face that brought up the paintings of Velasquez and Goya. Jason was taller than Rita's generation, well over six feet.

Sims was quick to make judgments about sexual preference, feeling his eye well-practiced after his time in London. There was no question that Jason was gay, but it could be many years before that was converted into action. Families in Santa Fe wanted their young men to marry, have children, with endless questions about when to expect a trip to the altar, after that when are the little ones due. We'll worry about proclivities later. A young, willowy lad had to be of strong mind and wily to escape that marital net. Sims would observe Jason's future with interest.

"Glad you're here, Jason. I've set up a table and chair for you in the kitchen room. There are several boxes of typing paper, and I see you've brought the Smith-Corona."

"Tanta Rita says you are a famous novelist."

"She exaggerates. I am working on a new book, the one you will be typing up for me. Let's get you going and see if you have problem with my handwriting. I have a few more chapters to go, but this is most of it. I'll be in the next room for questions. One original and one carbon copy."

Sims approved of the way Jason did not complicate things, getting right to typing in the next room. He certainly sounded like ninety-five words a minute right from the start, and Sims wondered if he himself would get used to the sound of typing going on while he was trying to think and write by hand in the next room. Shutting the door gently, he sat for a while considering. Maybe he should have Jason take home the work to type it up. He recalled a comment from a friend in London, that the difference between a journalist and a writer was that a writer worked alone in glorious silence and the journalist was only happy in the cacophony of a dozen typewriters, telephones ringing, people talking. One was seldom switched for the other, he also said.

Sims would try for a day or two to make this work. He unscrewed the cap to his black pen and got to writing. This was the chapter to start the complex process of ending the novel. His first-person narrator had experienced a spectacular rise in the banking world of Philadelphia, gone through innumerable personal problems to bring him down a bit, then after a retreat into the sylvan reaches of Appalachians, come back to face the world. He would meet face-to-face with his difficult father in this chapter, battling for control of the family firm. He wondered if the equally difficult mother was too-close a picture of his aunt, the rackety Augustine. Sims had a surprise in mind for the final chapter.

He thought the trials of a returning young veteran would again make a subject that the post-war reading public wanted to know, told in a different way from *The Mirror Shattered*. There must be tens of thousands of men going through this right now, finding their place in the economic explosion of the 1940s. This book was not organized around the broken mirror idea, but a customary, chronological story. Sims thought wistfully back to the days of writing of *The Mirror Shattered,* and he secretly wanted another project with an odd structure. Perhaps the next one.

The noon hour arrived, and Sims opened the door to the adjoining room. "Jason, let's go down to the house where Rita will have a lunch for us."

"Great, Mr. Sims."

"Please call me Sims."

"I think I can finish your work tomorrow."

"You're a marvel. You'll meet my partner Owen, the painter, and his new studio assistant, Oliver. We always stop for lunch."

SPAGHETTI SOUFFLÉ

Owen and Oliver were already at the table, which had four place settings, glasses of iced tea at each place, an empty plate, and a platter of assorted sandwiches, with slices of cheese and apples in the middle of the table. Rita made their lunches, usually for just Owen and Sims, as her first task of the day. Ham with cheese, egg-salad, cream cheese with watercress, or tuna salad were the usual fare. The work in the two studios was of sacred importance to both Rita and Perfecto, they serving as gatekeepers and protectors. Lunches were consistently light, usually the sandwiches, hard-boiled eggs, and tea, sliced fruit for dessert. She had arrived a bit earlier today to put together a fancier meal for the two guests.

"Spaghetti soufflé," she said as she brought the steaming hot dish wrapped in a tea towel, soufflé still standing up, and a gravyboat of tomato meat sauce. "Don't touch the hot dish."

Owen thanked Rita and served each of them a portion with a covering of the red sauce and a sprinkle of grated cheese. "This is Rita's specialty," he said.

"So you guys have this every day?" Oliver asked. "Like I died and went to heaven."

"Usually it's just a cheese sandwich and back to work," Owen replied.

"Still."

"I want to say," Sims said. "Jason got done in a morning what would take me more than several days to do. Let's have a drink of iced tea to that." They all raised their glasses.

"I don't want to work slowly," Jason said.

"Let me tell you what I have decided," Sims said. "I have read that Henry James had someone like Jason, who could work quickly. After ten or so novels were written the old way by hand, he thought he would try dictating his novels directly and the assistant would type along with him. It worked and all the rest of his books were made like that."

"Can *you* actually do that?" Owen asked.

"Tomorrow we're going to try. I have the outline of a chapter written, and we'll work from that."

"I wonder if you will start making sentences that go on forever. I remember having to slog through Henry James, whole pages without a period."

"I will take your warning to heart. Short and sour, more like Hemingway."

"Well, I think Oliver and I made some headway, too," Owen said.

"Yeah," Oliver said, "Owen got a painting almost finished this morning. Of me, by the way."

"So portraits will be on the docket?" Sims asked.

"In good time, you'll see," Owen replied.

Sims spent some time during the rest of the meal trying to make out what sort this Oliver Darge was. He was not the type that interested Owen in the past, too working class and broad-shouldered. Sims's thoughts sounded snobbish and wrong even in the privacy of his mind. He was almost sure there was no sexual interest there, so he wanted to see the new painting. Why would Oliver say it was of him?

"May we see your studio, Mr. Owen?" Jason asked.

"Please call me Owen. Yes, right after lunch, if Sims doesn't mind."

"Sims doesn't mind. We'll all go to see what he hath wrought."

They walked up to the painting studio in a group after lunch. The new painting was there on the easel, and Owen was happy to see that it was all he had remembered from the morning, strong and male. While Owen talked to the others, describing his method and what having a studio was about, Sims studied the new piece. It was wonderful, he thought. Owen truly has made the leap forward he so wanted. He could also see why Oliver said it was a portrait of him, because it was just that. There was an earthly maleness to the canvas, obviously coming from the muscled legs, but casting it all in a step back from reality. Owen's worry about a stalled career was over if this was the start of his new work. Sims wanted to hold him close with no words, but it would be too awkward with the others there. He must choose his words carefully, knowing the months of angst that had preceded this.

"You've turned the corner, sweetheart. It is what you wanted."

"I am too scared to be proud. I don't want to jinx it."

"Let's not, then. I'll come again in a couple of weeks, when it is done."

"You understand."

"The skin is too tender, too new."

Sims knew that a new painting was not so very much different from a new chapter in his book, a chapter with nuggets here and there, but needing to be polished, diminished, expanded, or just left alone. Only time could do that.

"So Jason, let's head up to my writing cottage and get to work. I promise not to channel Henry James."

Hank wondered when the physical attraction would wane, now that they had been together as a threesome for almost three years. In a few months it would be the anniversary of the night Sims bid him to join them in bed. If anything, the sensual joy was stronger and more rewarding now. He had learned the sensitive areas of each of their bodies and it gave him joy to turn them on, like a light switch bringing a warm light to a darkened room. The other two had reciprocated to find his special zones. Was love nothing more than a string of discoveries of those sensitive areas, until there were no more to discover?

When the three of them went out together to restaurants, Hank at first had been wary that others would see into their hearts, know that they were too much in love. But in Santa Fe, they were accepted as merely three good friends who were often seen together. Maybe it was beyond most people's imagination to think that three men could be lovers, while it was obvious when two men often together were gay. So they passed under the radar, no flashing heart-lights to give them away.

Sims had talked about the subject last night after dinner. "I suppose at some future time, our love will diminish, turn slowly cooler and cooler. We will probably all still be friends, but the sex part will not be there. We will go to others for sex. Is that what happens to all relationships?"

"I don't think it has to," Owen said. "As long as there is some mystery, some part of you that you are holding back, not letting me see, I think there is an attraction."

Hank knew he was right. Sims had the more curious mind, never giving an expected answer, which betold of another world that Sims could live in, without inviting Owen and Hank in. Was it a world where he was happier? And Owen had an occluded side as well, the other side of the moon that never turned around. It was always there, a whole half of him that Hank and Sims did not know. It was a natural, not self-conscious, aspect of each of them, but Hank could not help wanting to be part of those other worlds, too.

If he tried harder to love them, would they lift the curtain a bit, let him see what he had not? And there were many parts of Hank that Owen and Sims did not know, the thoughts that only a member of San Ildefonso can have, primordial thoughts, imbedded memories of long journeys through badlands. Probably all of the world's peoples had these memories, but they were closer to the surface in the pueblo people, part of a more recent past. As long as there were these shaded parts to each of them, there were mysteries swirling about.

Hank could enter their bodies, but he could never go beyond that semi-transparent wall that let a tantalizing glow come through, nothing definite but immensely tantalizing. There was something there, Hank knew, and his quest to know led him on. Maybe that was the engine of love, the push to know the unknown parts of the lover.

As he wrote every day, Sims thought a lot about love

and what it was, lately savoring the metaphor that it was a tree. He felt lucky to have this many-branched tree that was his, Hank and Owen, but he knew the limbs and branches went way away up into the darkness, so far he could no longer see even their outline. He could only stand by the trunk and look up, supposing he knew. There was so much darkness involved with love.

Maybe it was that love could not live in the full light, it needed a gloaming world to thrive, where imaginations and suppositions were their most comfortable. It was the edges of day instead of full noon. When the sun glared down on love, it wilted away. Sims remembered Owen talking about how the full sunlight could ruin a painting. It scorched it. He knew that a metaphor was his way to delineate truth, but it could also lead in the wrong direction. The tree still worked the best in his mind. Some of the branches were Owen, others were Hank, all of them going off so far he could not make out what they looked like. When would he know what the whole tree looked like, how far afield the branches went?

In this third year of their being together, Owen also thought about his two lovers as he worked at the easel. Being a visual person, he came up with graphic diagrams of what love was about. Of course, he knew the strength of an equal-sided triangle. It was a form from nature, a building block of life. Maybe they should change the name of Summerville House to Equilateral House. Were they actually equal? They tried hard to be equal and to view the others as equal. Maybe that was enough. However, if they were a right triangle, was he the hypotenuse, the one that held them together?

Owen continued to think if love were a color, it would

surely be green. Pale green as it started, unsure of itself. Eau de Nil. The milky green of mint Junket. Then, for the full summer of love, it would be deep green, apple green, viridian, sap green, Hooker's Green, Chromium Green, Jenkins Green, Phthalo Green, the deep color of foliage, butter lettuce, broccoli, asparagus, the green of abundance, the season of plenty, the salad days, with only a touch of yellow in late August. Yellow roses are for a dying love. Deeper yellow as the leaves start to fall.

If their love could be marked on the color chart, Owen thought, it would still be the apple green of full summer. That pleased him. Was it immutably necessary that the seasons went on, changed, lost strength, gave into the winds from the north? He remembered walking with his fatalistic father Isaac in the Appalachians of August. Owen's mother, Augustine, said that for Isaac there was always a storm on the horizon, black clouds just over his shoulder, not an entirely bad quality for an industrialist. Owen and Isaac went into the mountains each year in his teens, what a boy must do with his father, bonding in the actual depths of nature.

It was hot, insects buzzing, dust on the trail, haze on the distant foothills, and Isaac pointed out that in the crush of green there was always a touch of yellow in every tree. Perhaps only a single leaf among the tens of thousands, but there was one, somewhere. That was the winter, making her first mark, sitting still, saying notice me, notice me, but always in view. There would be more to come. It would not be summer forever. But, Owen thought to himself, it would be best to enjoy his own summer while it was here, the salad days with Hank and Sims, days that gave him great pleasure, often a explosion of pleasure, and not to search closely for that one yellow leaf.

UNCOMFORTABLE COUCHES

U nder Malvina's close eye, the refurbishing of their
house and studio in Menton came to a fine finish. The
house exterior was plastered and shutters repainted the de-
sired fern-green color, Alberta's painting studio brought
up-to-date with skylights and new windows, the stonework
on the olive and citrus terraces pointed or replaced, and the
pool on the lowest terrace brought back to a sparkling pale
blue with a single high arch of water into its very center,
almost a woodland glade on the Delphic coast.

She tried not to think about being bored, without a project, but it kept coming up in her mind. Was this all there
was? Would there be no more building projects? The Summerville School had always come forth with a new project, a crumbling wall or ceiling that showed water marks.
Malvina was happiest when the Grand Impasse resounded
with the clink of stonemasons at work, the chugging of
concrete mixers and the coarse language of workers calling
back and forth to each other. This new silence pressed in.

"Alberta," she said one morning as she came into the
studio, where the painter was sitting on a stool at the easel.
"I have an idea."

"That's dangerous, dear," she responded, slowly adding
a thin line of deep red to a storm cloud.

"Our house and studio are in fine fettle now, nothing more to do except to maintain it as time goes on. Guy Martel is a wonder, finding loose stones without my asking. I'm twiddling the thumbs."

"Oh, that reminds me, please ask Martel to fix my door. It squeaks, you know. Very annoying."

"I don't think you heard me, dear. This new idea concerns *me* and what to do with my time."

"You said often that you have started to write your memoirs."

"I have shelved that for now. I thought tomorrow we would take a drive along the coast to Le Cannet. An old house there is in need, right up the road from Pierre Bonnard's closed-up house."

"You've been reading the advertisement pages of *Nice-Matin* again," Alberta said, adding another red line.

"Shall we go?"

Alberta assented and they got up early the next day for the forty-five kilometer drive. Malvina had researched the property at the Menton library after reading the listing for sale. It was a white stone house, three stories with a mansard roof, built in the nineteenth century for a retired bank manager in Le Cannet, on a flat hectare of land just above the Canal de la Sciagne, which divided the upper town from its lower half. It was a white elephant in the midst of acres of the more traditional ground-hugging houses with red-tile roofs and small gardens. There was a short bit of open hilly land between Cannes and Le Cannet, the house nicely away from coast but said to have splendid views. And it was in deliciously bad repair, thus the notably lowered price. Twenty thousand francs.

Although not reported in the advertisement, Malvina

knew it was only a dozen houses away from the Bonnard villa, now boarded up and weedy since the painter's death two years ago. In time this would be a valuable neighborhood when the tight-pocketed French government started to honor their deceased painters. Malvina knew that Monet's house in Giverny had also become derelict, no public funding and general disregard for its welfare. Even Versailles, the very symbol of France's past, was in need of much repair. The post-war French were not stepping up to look after their abundant patrimony.

Most of the houses in Le Cannet had become seedy, the war years seeing many of the retired mid-level professionals gone, their houses in family fights, nobody finding the time or money to maintain or repair. Younger relatives did not want to live in the poorly heated houses from a century ago. The winter rains kept the trees and overgrown gardens alive, but the houses suffered. This was just the sort of project that inspired Malvina. Low price, heady possibilities. They stopped to view the Bonnard villa on the way up the hill. A chain-link fence had been installed all around it, with signs for no trespassing wired on every twenty feet.

"Oh, my gracious," Alberta said. "The French should be whipped or is it his family that needs punishment?"

"There are several Bonnard family lawsuits over who is the rightful heir. Of course, it's the odd old Uncle Pierre's now valuable paintings in a bank vault that they're haggling over, not this house. In the meantime the house gets totally neglected."

"Let's drive on, dear. It makes me sad."

"We'll see what the Auberon house looks like," Malvina said, putting the Hispano-Suizza into low gear. It was only a few minutes farther up the hill, an ornate gate in the wrought iron fence already opened up by the agents for the viewing. Malvina had telephoned the agent from her first sale in Menton, the M. d'Effron, to show it to them. He had arrived earlier and opened up the musty house. He stood by the front door.

"Mademoiselle Summerville, good morning."

"This house seems to be in even worse shape than the one we bought, Monsieur d'Effron. The land around it is generous, however, but the poor gardens. Let's walk through."

It was quite different from the country elegance of the Grande Impasse. High ceilings, ornate crown moldings, parquet floors. Some of the windows were broken, even the costly curved glass ones, and birds had deposited their droppings here and there. They toured the whole house, top to bottom. Malvina noticed that the high windows from the main floor salon had impressive views of the Mediterranean, a band of blue far down the hill, but a number of trees had grown up from their pleachings to block the view. They could be pruned down again.

"I like it, monsieur, but think a lower price is more appropriate. What do you think?"

"*Mais, oui.* These are not my clients as was the dear widow back in Menton. What price are you thinking about?"

"Knowing, like I do, that most buyers are terrified of renovating and its cost, I expect that only a very few people will be interested. It seems, also, that the whole of Le Cannet has grown a bit seedy, down at the heels since Bonnard's heyday, unlike our Menton. I suspect this house has been on the market a long time, even though the advertisement said otherwise. They are asking twenty thousand francs, so

I think a generous offer is fourteen thousand."

"I will submit such an offer and call you at your home in Menton."

"Good day, monsieur. You are a delight."

As they drove back to Menton, Alberta asked questions. "Do we intend to live in Le Cannet?"

"Not full-time, no. But perhaps on occasion. I thought to have it as a place for your art, where we can give receptions now and then. Houses from the Third Republic were made for receptions, all these tall rooms on the main floor. It would be a private gallery, more than a public one."

"My goodness, you have been thinking ahead."

"If we keep it going for ten years or so, I think it will have grown into a valuable asset. We can hang your paintings on those high walls, decorate it with a more modern touch than our Menton house. It will keep me from going crazy with inaction, my dear. The work will cost only twenty or so, to put it back together."

"You have a sense of these things, Malvina. I approve."

"May we rename it Villa Alberta?"

"Let me think about that first."

That was how the two ladies from Philadelphia started into the French fine art business, a move that should have been more obvious earlier on. The sellers of Auberon House asked for a small bit more money, which was accepted and the sale was completed. Malvina hired the same collection of men who had worked for her in Menton, letting them stay in the lower floors of the house until it was done, their wives coming over to join them on weekends. She made twice-weekly trips along the Grande Corniche to inspect and instruct. Most construction work in France at the time proceeded like the proverbial snail, but Malvina's villa project was done in five months, April through August. Her workmen clearly liked working for Malvina, the American wonder.

Uncomfortable low, white-upholstered couches were purchased for the main rooms, with cutting-edge side chairs and tables lining the walls where the paintings would not be hung. The dark oak paneling was painted an off-white throughout the house, at first bringing murmurs from the workmen. Wiring was redone so each painting had an individual light, making the paintings glow bright in the subdued lighting elsewhere. The glass doors with small balconies, locked shut for decades with encrusted paint, were opened for sea-breezes to flow through, new white linen draperies circling out. The highly patterned wood floors were refinished and polished, now dark and shiny. Dark walls became light, tawny floors became like ebony.

Malvina's construction workmen relished the installation of the paintings, a project they had never done before. They knew she was entrusting them with an enterprise several levels above their accustomed plasterwork and masonry. She paid them a bit extra for that. It was the end of September, and Auberon House had its first evening occasion. This time it was just for Alberta, Malvina, the workmen, and their wives. A good red wine was offered to all, with trays of small savory pastries, heated in the new modern kitchen downstairs and passed around by young women from the town. This try-out occasion was a grand success, so Malvina thought the villa was set for the winter season.

Good intentions might not be enough, as it turned out. The first public reception in early November was well-attended, a string quartet from Nice was hired to play Satie and Debussy tone-poems, and waiters circulated with trays of champagne flutes filled to the brims. Most of the paintings on the walls, now so very well illuminated, were painted by Alberta, but she had also decided to include three canvases of Pierre Frejus, now owned by a neighbor in Mention. It seemed right and of-a-piece since the paintings were all painted in the same studio in Menton. Alberta's canvases were a continuation of her Quasi-Realist Pueblo paintings series, the ones so well received in Paris.

All three of Frejus's post-impressionist paintings sold, but not a single one of Alberta's pieces. It was heard in nearby conversations that she was not French enough to collectors, too foreign. And one woman said, *What, indeed, was this thing, a pueblo?* All the champagne was consumed, however, as well as the many trays of succulent finger food. The waiters stayed late to clean up the salon room ashtrays and empty glasses. Igor de Foche came down from Paris for the occasion, weaving his sinuous way through the crowd, his Parisian black suit replaced by an impeccable white one with a black shirt and pointed black-and-white Italian shoes.

"I had hoped your American young p-p-people would be here again. *C'est dommage*," he told Alberta.

"You are dressed for the kill, but you must take a trip to New Mexico, Igor. To make your catch there," she said.

"Perhaps in the n-n-new year."

"I will write the boys that you inquired. They will be thrilled."

"Let's go home, sweetheart," Malvina said.

There would not be another reception at the Auberon House, they wisely deciding not to rename it Villa Alberta. It was late when they got back to Menton, both going to bed with only perfunctory conversation back and forth. Alberta never went back to the house in Le Cannet, but Malvina drove another half-a-dozen trips there, looking after maintenance of the house during the following winter. By early spring, M. d'Effron had found a buyer for Auberon House, an easier sell this time with its newfound modernity, and for Malvina's trust fund there was a small profit even after the agent's commissions. A hired van with all of Alberta's paintings followed her on the last trip back, slow progress through honking traffic lest an Alberta painting tilt away from the sides and fall in the van.

The next day Malvina started in her writing room the first efforts at a memoir.

She took pride in her handwriting for which a prize had been given in her schoolgirl days back in Philadelphia, the young Summerville girl so full of promise. Maybe her story started there, at the Pinetree Academy for Girls, a tale of a girl quite different from her cousins or peers. As she wrote, the thwarted builder and renovationist knew her work in that regard was merely on hold, not totally discarded. Writing was good, but building was better. There would be another house project.

DOUBLE-TONGUED

Prestor McCain had read hundreds of novels in their manuscript form, usually nothing more than a cardboard box full of three hundred typewritten pages, double-spaced. He loved the printed books themselves, but there was a lurking sense of excitement in a manuscript. There just might be the Great American Novel lurking in those pages. He felt a kinship with the hunter of diamonds in the hills of Arkansas, looking down with delight to see an apricot-sized, glistening mass uncovered in a recent rain. He was reading Sims Summerville's newest piece, again set in the Philadelphia of his own time.

McCain liked the way Summerville wrote, often very long sentences that flowed, he thought, like mountain streams, dependent clauses opening onto long lucid passages, not unlike clear pools, rocks below and small fish swimming, then changing to the staccato of shorter phrases with a race to a satisfying ending. McCain knew this rhythm was not by chance, but by design. Before the war, there was great delight in American writing of short sentences with no adverbs. It was thought they were masculine, forthright, truthful, and he championed them. With the passage of time, he was brought back to the Churchillian idea that the lengthy English sentence could be a Noble Thing, particularly when it wended its way through difficult, ornate passages to climb, step by step, to a clear and precise summation. As in politics, Winston's literary preferences had been voted back into power after a time in the wilderness.

Summerville's story itself was not new, but certainly of continued interest in this post-war world. It was a first-person tale of a man you liked immediately, not too full of himself and able to see the comedy of everyday life, including humor focused on the ways of his upper class, who saw none in themselves, whatsoever. Modern readers liked to see the sky dark with arrows being shot into patrician ranks, watching them shudder and fall. Summerville knew firsthand the world of family banks, the secrets that build up alongside the piles of money in underground vaults, and the missteps available to all the vulnerable people who inhabited that starched world behind the Doric façades.

The narrator could as well have been a Peloponnesian prince, feeling the increased weight of high position pressing down on his youth, threatening to make him old before his time. And the solution, as always, was an odyssey away through danger, a testing time filled with odd creatures, adventures in sharp places, and the resolution of a troublesome trek away from and back to home-base. Several chapters described the healing process from the talon-wounds or the fall from great heights.

Was it possible to always find a myth imbedded behind the modern story, even if the writer of today knew nothing of it, but had only tapped something deep in his very bones that told the story? Was there something in the water of ancient Athens that went right into the cells of western mankind, staying there, making patterns, creating stories by writers now several hundred generations beyond? Prestor was sure there was.

The novelist himself was due for an interview, and right on time, there was a knock.

"Welcome again, Sims."

"Thanks for reading this, Prestor."

They walked over to the club chairs that faced each other by the fireside. Sims noticed that Prestor was now walking with a bamboo cane, the years making their mark. He wished that he would age this way, the mind staying crisp and alert, and if it had to happen, the body taking all the damage from the slings and arrows. Something must be given up to the greedy gods for a continued existence, so let it be the wide-paced stride.

"I always thought it was wise to discuss the good qualities of a project first," Prestor said. "To make the writer stop the clenched-fist nerves of letting someone else see his manuscript. I'll just say that I very much like your story, then we'll go on to the problems. Mostly technical, I must say."

"I wondered if you would see something."

"I had a witty friend who said there are only two stories in all of the literature of the world. Man or Woman Has Troubles, Makes Good. Man or Woman Has Troubles, Does Not Make Good."

"I would agree."

"Happily, we are dealing with the former one in your project. Although the world has little patience with tragedy now, there is an enduring place for it. You have created some harrowing adventures for your narrator, dangers no one could imagine lurked in fusty old Philadelphia. Even in the back rooms of a simple bookstore. Very compelling."

"That was the fun part."

"What do you think an author's voice is, Sims?"

"Hard to describe. I can certainly tell the difference between Dickens and Jane Austen, if you gave me a page of each of them. But I can't say why."

"That's voice. The manner in which you talk, how you space the words, the syncopation of the words together, the words themselves. The short interspersed with the many-syllabled, and on and on."

"I understand."

"There is a change in your voice near the end of your story. The first part is very similar to your previous book, long handsome sentences that almost disappear into themselves, a story being told in a craftsman-like way. We cannot see you working the strings when the puppets dance. Then a different, almost haranguing voice is heard, maybe like what the old writers described as the Oracle of Delphi's voice, shrill, double-tongued, two people intoning at the same time."

"That sounds annoying."

"It is to me, and I think it would be to many other perceptive readers."

"Where does it start?"

McCain thumbed through the pages and found the beginning of the last three chapters. Sims knew it was exactly when he started dictating the work to Jason.

"I can rewrite the last three chapters."

"Good. Otherwise it is ready to go. It is never wrong to take an underlying Greek myth and do filigree work upon it. They are even now strong and steady bases for modern fiction, particularly if the reader is not aware of what sort of footings lurk below the floor."

Sims thought it better that he did not divulge the dictating reason behind the rewrite. He would have to tell Jason that dictating was not working out. He knew Owen and Hank would be amused when at dinner that night he told them Prestor accused him of turning into a strident oracle, decreeing curses and bad outcomes from on high. A literary harpy. He loved talking to Prestor, or more exactly, listening to Prestor, even if he left his French library with a substantial head wound and assorted bruises.

Sims took a week to rewrite the last thirty pages, and in the process it was clear the difference between a mind talking and a mind writing. He decided that the writing mind was more thoughtful, more self-edited, maybe clearer than an outpouring of spoken words with no filter. That might explain why Henry James was so hard to read, why he never had the great commercial success of Edith Wharton, who wrote everything longhand. And did she write with an earlier model of his fountain pen from Switzerland, black ink on unlined, white paper?

He changed the title of his book to *The Uttermost Parts of the Sea* to give it a sense of Greek gravitas, even though it was a biblical quote, and mailed it to New York. Small and Redd wrote right back that it would be printed in time for the fall lists, an important window, and included an advance check. There was an invitation to come to New York for the publishing announcement party in early November, a fully laid-on cocktail party in the publisher's boardrooms. All of literary Manhattan would be there. Sims thought Owen and Hank must go there with him, have a metropolitan change from the innocent, and sometimes boring, happiness at Summerville House.

In the meantime Sims needed to find a different place

for Jason to work. He wondered if Prestor McCain was the answer, since he was the one who made it impossible to proceed with dictating a novel. There would be no need to confess to the dictation fiasco.

He answered the telephone simply, "McCain."

"Hello, Prestor. Sims here. I have a favor to ask."

"Of course."

"Jason Sanchez is the young man who types up my novel from the handwritten pages. He needs a place until something opens up at the courthouse or until I finish a handwritten new work."

"Say no more. I have need of him here."

"He has his own Smith-Corona and claims a faultless ninety-five words a minute. I'll ask him to come by your house."

"Tomorrow would be fine."

Sims thought of his mother and her dictum for young boys, *If you make a mess, you clean it up.* There you are, mother, an unfortunate bit on the floor cleaned up again by the dutiful son.

POTTED CHRYSANTHEMUMS

The months after a novel is finished and before it is actually published can be difficult for a writer, even if it is on a fast track, and Sims was no exception. Although he had the idea in his mind for the next novel, it was unformed and not ready for the light of day or any actual work. The short story seemed the answer for Sims, a project with a length of days instead of months. There were several stories in his mind about a boys' summer camp in the Poconos, stories that he and Owen had lived firsthand when they were in their early teens. A series of four stories was what Sims had in mind, each a tale of young sensuality coming into bloom, being thwarted in various ways, then pushing through to what appeared to the narrators to be first love. Sims was sure that everybody had experienced those spring days of love, the crocus pushing up into the sunlight from the last remnants of snow. He would ask Owen for ideas to add to his own.

The four stories were finished by the time he, Hank, and Owen were scheduled to fly to New York City to attend the announcement reception for *The Uttermost Parts of the Sea*. Sims slid the typewritten stories, each with its own paperclip, into the pocket on the top cover of his suitcase, hoping he would find a magazine to publish them. At the reception there could well be some magazine editors in attendance who might be open to such a suggestion.

Jacob Bourne was Sims's editor at Small and Redd, and he suggested they stay at the Barchester Hotel near the publisher's offices in Midtown. They could then walk over to the Friday night reception in the boardrooms. Jacob asked Sims to arrive no later than four-thirty to meet the first arrivals, and plan to stay until well after eight. Jacob also said that this was their first and most important party of the fall.

Hank, Owen, and Sims had each brought a black suit to wear, knowing that it was the only color for New York. Hank and Owen wore white shirts and ties, but Sims thought he would forgo the tie and unbutton the shirt's top button, the author evidencing a free spirit.

"You're going to knock 'em out, sweetheart," Owen said.

"It's odd," Sims answered. "I'm not nervous at all."

"Me, neither," Hank said, "because if we can get through that opening for Alberta in Paris like we did, I think New York will be a pushover."

"Maybe Igor will be there, flown in from Paris, pursuing the one he lusts year after year for."

"I should just say yes, get it over with."

"I'll l-l-look out for you," Sims said.

The three of them arrived on time when there were just a few of the publishers' people standing about. A photo enlargement of the book's cover stood propped up on the boardroom table with a circle of potted chrysanthemums around it, a full bar off to the side with three waiters standing by. Jacob Bourne walked over to greet them.

"Get ready, Sims, we expect there will be a large crush. The word is out that the great new novel has this very handsome author. I don't think the New York book crowd will be disappointed."

"You're sweet to say that, Jacob, and you're making me nervous."

They started in twos and threes, trickling in, heading straight for the bar, talking in clusters. The groups got larger as people continued to arrive, finally squeezing around the whole table, almost everybody smoking as well. Although Sims refrained from wearing the offered nametag, most of the guests figured who the author was and came by for a chat. For a while Hank stayed near, but found a chair on the side of the room next to Owen.

"Our boy is a hit," Hank said.

"He could have a very active life in New York," Owen said. "But I can tell that he is ready to leave. I'm going to wait for about twenty minutes more, then go over and say Mr. Summerville is needed elsewhere."

Jacob Bourne came to sit with Hank and Owen. "Tell me about your life in Santa Fe," he said. "Sims has talked a bit about it in our phone conversations. I would love to visit this winter, see for myself."

"We have a couple of spare rooms, so why don't you come at Christmas? I know Sims would love to have you, so I don't speak out of turn."

"I just may take you up on that, Owen. I have a partner, so there would be the two of us."

"Please invite him, too."

An older woman with a pile of gray hair and an admirable nose came up to Sims as he was talking to two men. She waited until Sims turned away from the men, their conversation complete.

"Hello, I'm Sims Summerville."

"Mary Louise Aston. I'm the fiction editor at Jordan's Bazaar."

"Jacob has talked about you. So pleased you came today."

"I'll get right to the point. I much admired your first book, *The Mirror Shattered*. May I have a story from you, anytime this winter?"

"Of course. I brought some new stories with me, hoping to find a home for them. Maybe I can ask Jacob to bring them by your office?"

"Perfect. I'll write to you after I read them."

"Prestor McCain hoped I could talk with you."

"We all listen when Prestor McCain calls. He was right to do so, and I'm coming out to Santa Fe. I visit my dear friend, Agnes Tibbs, more often now. We can talk then."

"I'm not sure that Jordan's Bazaar is the place for my stories, about young men and their days at summer camp."

"Let me decide that, Sims."

Sims watched as Mary Louise walked over to join one of the groups, who readily opened up a place for her. He was excited his stories would be considered, even though the subject was not in step with a fashion magazine. Others that were more suitable could be written if they were not. He looked over at Owen, who without words picked up the message that it was time to go. Saying no goodbyes, the three men left the reception. It was the wordless departure they practiced at parties back in Santa Fe, referred to as the Indian Rope Trick. Listo? Whoosh.

Two days in New York followed. The matinee of a new play, the Matisse exhibit at the Museum of Modern Art, two different Italian restaurants, several gallery shows of new painters, and a lunch at the Russian Tea Room with Jacob Bourne filled them. The next day was the flight to Dallas and on to Santa Fe. The country mice had become city mice for a moment, now breathing a sigh as they reached the Summerville House gates. As they drove through them Sims said to himself that even though the writing world needed New York, he knew now he could never leave the west. It was now in his blood.

The writing world would just have come to him.

HARVEST MOON

The canvases that Owen had been working on all winter, the legs of Oliver paintings, were virtually finished, in stacks against the walls of his studio house. He stayed with black and white paint, with all shades of gray in between, but no other colors. His technique became more refined, what had been long washes of color with a wide brush were now converted to masses of thin parallel lines, and a counterpoint of stronger lines dividing sections of the canvas. The motif of maleness continued, muscles and sinews that appeared like old anatomical prints gone haywire, filling the whole canvas with design. Entire sections of the work had accidental drippings down the canvas, as if a liquid were actually emerging from the surface of the painting. It would be impossible for anyone to not perceive the sensual quality of them all. Owen had gone well beyond those first charcoal sketches, inserting smaller patterns within the grand ones, placing reticulated lines against areas of smoothness. They were elegant paintings as well as strong.

Owen stayed with the six-foot by six-foot canvas, all of this series the exact same size. There was an empty house up the hill nearby his studio, which he took over to be his own display gallery. It had been a storeroom before, with small windows and many unpunctuated walls. He repainted the walls a pale warm gray, a mix of lamp black, a small bit of yellow ochre, and white. An electrician friend of Hank's added overhead lights and the cool colors of Owen's paintings all but jumped off the warm walls.

This was the harvest, Owen thought, the coming together. There were a dozen of the square panels, widely spaced throughout the building. Bringing some paints over to the new house, he continued painting upon them as he saw places that needed attention.

Owen showed the small gallery to Sims and Hank, they all walking up with wineglasses one evening. The lights were already on as they walked in, Owen setting the stage in advance. Neither of the other two men said anything as they stood before each painting in turn, walking slowly around the building. They knew this was a very important moment for their lover.

Sims formulated a comment in his mind, then discarded it. Owen's work would be still tender for him, he knew. There was never a chance to redo a hasty first comment, so Sims walked around.

Owen sensed the difficulty his lovers were having, fearing any comment might injure him or be seen as belittling his work. He would speak first.

"Mr. Holdings-Brown said that a painting is never done, the painter just stops working on it. He told of Pierre Bonnard taking his paints under his coat into a museum. Then, while his wife, Marthe, diverted the guards, he painted spots of new color here and there, trying to undo what he thought was unfinished."

"Are you happy with them?" Sims asked.

"Pretty much."

"I think they are wonderful."

"I showed them to Larry Fulton this afternoon. He grew excited about them and wants an exhibit in his gallery, but he's going to repaint all the walls this same gray color beforehand. They'll be ready by early September."

"Fulton's will be a good place to show them," Sims said. "Not much light from the street. By the way, do you think these paintings belong in artificial, electric light?"

"Completely. That's why I did this sample display."

"Owen, it is impressive," Hank said.

It was difficult for Hank to talk about art, deeper water than he was accustomed to. He knew that his eye for it was improving and that Owen's series would be taken seriously when the Fulton exhibit went up. He decided silence was best.

They turned off the lights and walked back to Summerville House. Owen thought his feelings were mixed about the project being so nearly complete. Farmers must feel that way when the last wheat has been trucked away, the stubble fields going off into the distance. It was both a sense of emptiness, the harvest taken away into the hands of others, and fullness, the accomplishment of six months creating art that had not been in existence before.

BY THE WINDOW, AGAIN

The three lovers had been together for seven years, and Hank was now the one who tried to assess the status of love. He knew there was a security in loving and being loved, a stable, small world encircled by a large world of insecurity and unknowns. If everything collapsed around them, the three of them would still be there. In other people, it was what family was to them, a safe island in the swirling, unreliable waters of the outside world. But there was a part of Hank, maybe the San Ildefonso part, that suspected the worst when times were too good. It was the same as that very still day in autumn that always presaged a month of storms. Life was too good.

Several years ago, Owen had reworked the two small bedrooms at Summerville House into a place for Hank. There were now three master bedrooms that interconnected, each one with an easy access to the other two. Rita had a sense about when to knock and when not to, but anyone else was faced with the great brass knocker in the shape of an upside-down dolphin on the door to the bedroom wing. It was their island within an island, the most sanctum of inner sanctums. No one else was welcomed.

They had finished dinner while it was still light outside and were sitting on the front portal, discussing the matters of the last few days. A matte-gray sedan came through the gates and parked in front of the portal. Owen could see it was a military vehicle, the driver sitting still while a man came out of the back seat. Although he was in civilian clothes, Owen thought he recognized the stiff military bearing as the man came up the few steps to the portal.

"Owen Parcher, you haven't changed at all," the man said.

"Why it's Major Arrowsmith, from the third floor in London."

"Colonel Arrowsmith now, in his civilian clothes."

Owen introduced him to Sims and Hank and asked him to sit down and join them. Sims asked if he would like something to drink and went to get him a simple seltzer and ice. He also took the same out to the driver in Army uniform, still behind the wheel. Sims saw that there was something Arrowsmith wanted to discuss with Owen in private.

"Hank and I will take our evening walk. Nice to meet you, Colonel."

"So, Owen. I've read the reviews on your painting career. A fine, new regional talent, says Art News."

"I'm surprised you read Art News. I wonder why?"

"As you might know, I stayed on with the OSS, now converted to the CIA. We keep up with all our promising former officers."

"Then, why me?"

"There is a mission that asks for an officer with a very particular set of requirements. He needed a former top-secret clearance, some knowledge of counter-intelligence, and an unquestioned reputation in publications as a top modern painter. Guess who fits those?"

"Surely there are plenty of others."

"Nope. Just one. I was so happy when I saw your name. You have the opportunity to do something really valuable for the nation."

"Patriotism makes me nervous, Peter. May I call you Peter, now that I'm not still in the service?"

"Please do. We will be working together. You might re-member our times in London."

"I remember them well. But, Peter, I have to tell you that I am homosexual. Been living with two lovers for the last several years. Not suitable, I believe, for your secret mission."

"We already know that. My people have run quiet in-vestigations of Hank and Sims, as well. Nothing irregular there, as far as we can see."

"You'll have to give me the details of your project."

Arrowsmith described what he wanted Owen to do for his country. The US State Department would buy a group of Owen's paintings, to be displayed with other artists in the Royal Academy in London, an international show lat-er this year to be part of the Festival of Britain. One of the other artists invited will be Leonid Ulensky, the most favorite painter of Soviet high command. In Moscow he painted many portraits of top generals and their wives. His paintings hung in the more important embassies, symbols of the excellence of loyal Soviet men in all the arts and sci-ences. They were all very traditional paintings, abstraction not available from Moscow. Owen would meet Ulensky — who the CIA had discovered is a very secret, but active, homosexual — at the reception at the Royal Academy and convince him to defect to the west. It would be a public re-lations coup for America, at a delicate time when the Soviet way seemed to be winning on all fronts.

"So you think one queer can easily convince another to defect? Perhaps with the lure of sexual favors?"

"We wouldn't expect actual contact, perhaps only teasing. And, of course, your exact natures would be kept secret."

"I can't help but laugh at your naïve understanding of how the pansy world, as you probably call it, operates."

"What we wish is that you and Sims go to London, attend all the parties, be your attractive selves. Make friends with the other artists, including Ulensky. Invite him to your place here in Santa Fe, to see what the art world of the US is really like."

"And then convince him to betray his own nation? To defect?"

"That's about it. My budget is thirty thousand dollars for your paintings, plus all expenses in London. It would be a massive defeat for the Soviets to have Ulensky come over to the west. We plan for a sorry summer for Russia, because there are plans under way for several other defections as well. What do you say?"

"I'll have to think, Peter, and ask Sims and Hank. By the way, if I do agree, Hank comes along too."

"Then, it's as good as done, Owen."

"There is some irony in that we would be encouraging Ulensky to defect to the west, where being a queer is illegal. Years in prison."

"It's a death penalty in Moscow."

"Okay, okay. I'll tell you tomorrow. By the way, how do you know that Ulensky is queer?"

"We have handsome agents."

"You mean deceptive, handsome agents."

Hank and Owen had timed the return from their walk

perfectly, coming down the driveway as the gray sedan approached the gate. Arrowsmith waved to them from the back seat as he passed by. At the portal, Owen asked them to sit down. As he told them the lengthy story, Sims was as amused as Owen had been, but Hank was stunned.

"Owen," he said, "it seems so unethical, not patriotic at all."

"I agree," Sims said. "It would be fun to go back to London, though."

"Let me think about it overnight," Owen said. "I'll decide by morning."

Owen slept better than the other two, each of them going to their own bedrooms. He got up early to cook a breakfast — scrambled eggs and bacon, toast and coffee.

He was waiting at the stove as they came in.

"Have some coffee first, then I'll tell you."

"You're not going to do it, are you?" asked Hank.

"See what you think. For the inconvenience of it all, I'll let the State Department buy four paintings at my regular prices, not that thirty thousand dollars. Then, we three get an all-expenses-paid first-class trip to London for the Royal Academy. I would love to see my paintings there, meet the other artists. We will meet this Ulensky and ask him to lunch with us, maybe at the Ritz dining room again. We will describe our life as artists in Santa Fe and invite him to visit. That's the sum of it. Nothing dishonest. If he accepts our invitation, we will still not inveigle him to defect or even so much as suggest it. If he defects, he will have to do it on his own. The CIA will have to take it or leave it."

"I guess there's nothing amiss with that," Hank said. "Do you think including Viona would start to push the ethics of the matter?"

"I can make a case that it would make our cover more authentic," Owen said.

"London, here we come," Sims said.

"I'll ask Arrowsmith to make the lunch reservations for five of us at the Ritz. By the windows. Could be a crowd of tourists there, what with the Festival of Britain."

"It still seems somehow off-key to me," Hank said. "But I don't see anything actually illegal. Owen, you never talked about what you did in the war. Were you a spy?"

"I was called an Analyst, no dangerous missions in the field."

"Could this one be dangerous?"

"I don't see how. I remember a cynical French proverb that went around the London office. *It is a double pleasure to deceive the deceiver.*"

"You have had a very shadowy past, Owen."

"More desk work than work in the field."

"I somehow doubt that."

"No assassinations, however."

Viona's dress shop continued as a successful business. She was able to hire assistants to run the shop, giving her more time to spend with her friends. At the end of each December, she paid the equal partners Rita and Owen their share of the profit and caught the aunts up on what was owed them. At one of the Saturday dinners, she took her friend Sophia de la Pena, a new artist in town. It was natural that her time with Hank had been lessened as his focus turned to Owen and Sims. There was no jealousy or unhappiness in this because Viona had always known that Hank was not for her. She was not sure who was for her, however, a man or a woman.

She met Sophia at an art opening across the street from her La Fonda shop. It was one of the first galleries in Santa Fe, run by a woman named Margaret Jennison. Margaret had developed a friendship with Viona, both women loving the ins and outs of fashion. They had lunch together and sometimes went to concerts. Each knew that a successful businesswoman needed to be seen about town, and each was proud to be seen with the other. Margaret was insistent that Viona come to this opening reception.

Sophia was younger than Viona, with darker Spanish looks: her jet-black hair worn long to below the shoulders, black-brown eyes, and the often paint-covered hands of a committed painter. She came from the small village of Can-jilon north of Santa Fe, but instead of moving back home after her university days, she rented a small house in the barrio just south of the river. It had a studio and three other rooms, perfect for a single artist. A committed painter, she turned down dates from both men and women to work late at night. Margaret Jennison gave her a first solo show, and that opening reception was where Viona met Sophia.

"I'm Viona Maes. From the shop across the street."

"I want one of your dresses."

"Please come by. Say tomorrow. Just before lunch?"

"May I bring Margaret, too?"

"No, just you and me. I have the black dress perfect for you."

"All right."

There was an intensity about Sophia that fascinated Viona, who then watched her from afar at the opening reception, talking to collectors and art regulars. Viona could see Sophia glancing over at her as she talked to admirers, still showing to Viona the intensity she had not seen in her male friends. Sophia had dark eyebrows, which she moved up and down while talking, making a point with them as they went up to their zenith. Viona could not sleep well that night, thinking about Sophia's visit to her shop the next day. There were popular songs about seeing a love first from afar, across a busy room, and now it had happened to her, the beautiful face in her mind like a tune she could not forget.

Their friendship progressed from the gift of the black dress to the gift of one of Sophia's paintings in return, a self-portrait of her in tears, a storm in the window behind her. All of her paintings were personal and dramatic versions of a woman suffering, sometimes of a woman yelling. Viona thought Sophia would become an important painter.

They had several lunches together, then several dinners together. Sophia asked Viona if she would like to come to her small house south of the river for a home-cooked dinner, like they made in Canjilon. Then, after several of those, Viona asked to spend the night, the aroma of turpentine still in her clothes as she went to her shop the next day.

Sophia was not an easy catch, however. After several weeks of passionate togetherness, she asked Viona to stay away for a while. Viona saw her with another woman in the Jennison Gallery across the street, a tall blonde woman who looked like one of her dress customers from Texas. Viona could not watch them too closely as she had customers to attend to. There was an ache in her body all the time for Sophia. Then she saw Sophia with a man, who she told herself was her favorite brother from Canjilon whom she had talked about. But the way he put his arm around her did not look like a brother's hug, after all.

Hank saw that Viona was hurting at the Saturday dinner at Summerville House, only the four of them. Owen and Sims were talking about family matters back in Philadelphia.

"Oh, honey, I can feel your hurt," he said.

"I don't know what to do," she answered.

"Nothing. It will go away in time."

"There is a man who came into the shop today. He said he has been seeing me around town, and could we go out together for dinner?"

"But you came here instead."

"He said he would come back again. He is handsome."

"Maybe our trip to London will help you forget Sophia."

Viona did not forget Sophia, but she did go to dinner with Martin. He met her at the shop and drove her up Canyon Road to the Compound Restaurant. At first she did not talk about Sophia, but the business at the shop. He seemed to be interested in business matters in general and those of her shop in particular. Then she thought, if I cannot be truthful with Martin, this is not going to work out.

"Martin, I have something to say. I love a woman who does not seem to love me."

"That must hurt a lot."

"It does, and that is why I am not good company tonight. I can't get her out of my mind as I talk to you."

"I'm glad you told me."

"Have you ever loved someone that way?"

"I also loved a woman who did not love me. Yes."

Viona thought that Martin was a patient man, a man who could be good to her. The conversation turned to other topics and Martin started with diffidence of telling about himself. From a California family who owned a stretch of coastline, he grew up in and out of the surf. He wanted to write a history of that family after he moved to Santa Fe, and he worked on that every day. She wanted to ask what he did for money, but decided he would tell her in time. When he put his hand on hers, as he often did during their dinner, she felt a strength in him, as well as a sensual rush. That must be a good sign.

Time went by and Viona had not seen Sophia going in or out of the Jennison Gallery. Margaret Jennison told her that Sophia had left her paintings at the gallery and was driving with a friend to Mexico. They might or might not be back. Viona could not get up the courage to ask if the friend was a man or a woman, but either way it appeared to be the end.

She continued to go out with Martin, still not giving herself away. Martin said he was fine with that, she was worth the wait. When she got back from the trip to London with Hank, Owen, and Sims, she would make a decision. Since Martin was here and Sophia was not, it should have made the choice easy, but Viona knew that either way, there would always be teasing voices in her head describing the delights that could have been.

A SHORT WALK DOWN PICCADILLY

The exhibit at the Royal Academy held its morning grand opening on the week after Easter, well before the main activities of the Festival got under way. Owen thought the sponsors of the exhibit had planned well to avoid the festival itself as competition. The four of them from Santa Fe had arrived earlier and were rested, ready for the private opening. Their reservations at the Ritz dining room were on for a one o'clock lunch afterwards.

"I'm anxious to meet Leonid and get this affair over with," Owen told the others as they walked into the front courtyard of the Academy.

"Let's try to stay together, because I see a crush of people inside," Sims said.

Owen was given a nametag at the door, while the others were checked off the official guest list. The actual exhibit was several rooms away from the entry hall, so Owen led them in single file through the many standing groups. He wondered if all of British Intelligence was there in their finery, talking art with their flutes of morning champagne but on the lookout for other operatives from all sides of Europe.

If brushwork and color choices were on their lips, defection to the west was on their minds. The London papers reported that a noted nuclear scientist had switched sides just

a few days before, hiding under a pile of cabbages being de-
livered to West Germany. Arrowsmith's project was already
under way. Owen kept moving forward in the crowd, thinking how different Britain was from their provincial society.
At art openings in Santa Fe, he had never sensed these many
layers of undercurrents, people saying one thing and thinking quite another. In a way, it was exciting, the danger pal-
pable. The Soviets would be furious if they lost Ulensky and
would they seek revenge, an oddly dressed woman in stout
shoes with a hidden pistol walking down the front drive to
Summerville House with an umbrella on a summer day?

"Here we are," he said to the others, pointing to his four
canvases, hung together in a wide-spaced row. "They look
okay."

"They look beautiful, sweetheart," Viona said. "We're
so proud." The three men had not informed her of the clandestine reasons for their attendance, only the fact that their
Owen was now receiving international exposure.

Owen spotted Leonid Ulensky next to his paintings
across the room, in a small circle of men in double-breasted
suits. Leonid was dressed in a wrinkled suit of light gray,
standing out from the others. Owen's first impression was
how much Leonid resembled their Hank, strong stance and
broad shoulders, legs slightly apart, talking with his hands,
large hands like Hank, and the same square face, dark eyes
and hair. He wondered if the others saw the resemblance,
leading them to penetrate the circle surrounding the Russian painter.

"Leonid, I am Owen Parcher from Santa Fe."

"Hello, my friend. We have much to talk about."

"You know you have a place at our lunch table, in about
an hour?"

"I've been told. I'll be there."

"I want to look at your paintings and we'll talk later."

Sims, the man who relished what happened behind the fan, wondered why it was not completely obvious to the Soviet higher-ups that Leonid was homosexual. It was obvious to him as he watched the hand movements and stance of the Russian. Leonid was not effeminate, but Sims knew there was another Leonid underneath the one he showed to the world. Maybe it was a curse to see so closely, Sims thought. How nice to believe there was solid white marble behind such facades, thinking the best. He also wondered if Leonid knew that he was living precariously on borrowed time, that a defection may be his only way out of a public unmasking and death. He should act like French aristocrats fleeing early before the guillotine held sway, the only ones who survived.

It was very hard to see the other paintings, the crowds of people now so close by. Owen's group stayed with him as he gently said, *"Excuse me,"* again and again. He had attended enough opening nights at Santa Fe galleries to know the procedure. They looked through the other painters' offerings this way, prising an opening between the people, and after an hour or so, slowly made their way out towards the front door. Owen said his goodbyes to the officials there.

It was Sims who knew the way to the Ritz Hotel, a short walk down Piccadilly. Their reservation was a table for six by the windows. The view across Green Park now lived up to its name, the tall shade trees all in late spring leaf, a few flowering trees sheltered between them. The French windows were left ajar with a light breeze moving the cigarette smoke.

"We're waiting for another guest, a Mr. Ulensky," Owen

told the headwaiter. "But I can order from your wine list while we wait."

"Leonid looked somehow familiar, when we met him," Hank said.

"Silly, he looks just like you," Viona said.

"He does? I don't see it."

"Well, let's see what he thinks."

Leonid arrived and took the chair next to Owen, leaving the last chair next to him vacant. Everybody reintroduced themselves as the white wine was being poured into their glasses. Owen told the waiter to order two more bottles. He saw that the three men in black suits who accompanied Leonid were sitting at a cheerless table not far away, and at a table just beyond them was Arrowsmith with his own group, equally unsmiling. Viona, who was looking the other way, laughed as she pointed to a table with a man and woman.

"Gracious, it's Igor and his sister from Paris. What a coincidence. Look."

A warning shot through Owen's mind. He remembered the words form his short training in the OSS. There are *no* coincidences in counter-intelligence. Always pay attention, something is afoot. Igor saw Viona pointing and came over to kiss her on the forehead. Martine de Foche waved discreetly but stayed at her table.

"So exciting, this L-L-London art world."

"Sit down for a bit," Owen said.

"Just for the moment."

"Mr. Ulensky, I need to t-t-talk with you," Igor said. "May I sit down next to you?"

Leonid assented and the chatter between them all grew. Owen could not hear everything that Igor said, but he heard enough to know Igor wanted to show Ulensky's artwork in the gallery in Paris. He would guarantee sales. Owen surmised that this was the French version of his own counterintelligence sortie in the Royal Academy, a ruse to switch the defection of Ulensky to France rather than the US. Did the French pick their operatives from the art world rather than the English way, only the young men from Oxford or Cambridge? It was suitably French, determined to be different, to grant artists top-secret clearances instead of the tweedy students from university classics departments. Their ship was nearing its destination, Owen knew.

Was the CIA aware of this turn as a French effort? He looked over at Arrowsmith's table and saw the Colonel looking intently their way. This might be an answer to the worry Owen could not dispel about this endeavor, the ethics behind all the falsehoods. It was also the way for the famous Indian Rope Trick for his group from Santa Fe.

"Leonid, you must take Igor up on his offer," Owen said. "My aunt's companion, the painter Alberta Todd, had a Paris show with Igor and his sister, and it made her name in Western Europe. She said she would have been forgotten without them. Galerie de Foche was the very center of the French art world."

"S-S-Such kind words, Owen," Igor said, with a quizzical look on his face. "But they could well be true."

"I can almost say yes right now," Leonid said. "I have wanted to exhibit in a private gallery in Europe. The Royal Academy is good, but not for the commerce."

"There you have it, Igor," Owen said. "As good as done."

Owen knew he would have to update Arrowsmith on these developments. Saying he saw somebody he needed to say hello to, Owen left the table and walked over to Arrowsmith's table.

"I think our man will move to Paris, instead."

"Didn't you invite him to Santa Fe?"

"No need. As I told Igor, it's as good as done. Contract fulfilled."

"Do it anyway, just in case. We'll get back with you, Parcher."

As he walked back to the table, Owen saw Leonid and Igor talking intently in lowered voices, while Viona and Hank were talking together, and Sims winked across to him a knowing wink. They must order lunch before the wines took away their good sense. He also knew with a sense of relief that his re-entry into the world of counterintelligence had been more than just put on hold, it had been cancelled, and that more quiet days of Summerville House were soon ahead, where deceit did not take root so easily.

"Leonid, after your Paris visit, you are welcome to come to us in Santa Fe," Owen said as he was ordered to do. "We have an odd, but active art scene there. Small, but choice. Just give us a ring."

Leonid nodded with a smile, but said nothing while standing up to go. As if the queen herself had stood to indicate departure, the three at the Russian table, the four at the Arrowsmith table, and Martine de Foche all stood up as well. The luncheon of all possibilities was over, fate veering them all into a different direction than planned. The motley crowd of people headed as a group for the exit doors, chatting among themselves. British onlookers must have thought them merely impolite festival-goers, yet another odd foreign group.

On their flight home, Hank sat next to Owen. "Igor barely said hello to me. It was good not to have his eyes on me."

"Or his hands. Be thankful."

"But your Leonid is another matter."

"What did he do?"

"Nothing, really, just the way he looked at me. I'm
learning from Sims."

Owen felt glad that this sortie was coming to its close.
When he was younger and in the OSS in London, he had
been excited about the ins and outs of counterintelligence,
involved and edgy episodes that were clearly related to the
winning of the war. The officers made a point of describing how a single letter, formulated in their office and attached innocently onto the underside of a Hyde Park bench,
brought down the top Nazi admiral, the one who had been
so effective with his submarines in the Atlantic. Like a well-
directed arrow, the allied deception made its way across to
Berlin, hinting at the mere chance of betrayal and causing
chaos and indecision for an important moment or so, long
enough for a convoy of munitions ships to slip safely into
Liverpool. The hint itself was enough.

Now, under the indistinct, fuzzy mantle of patriotism
against the Soviets, the worth of such duplicity was open
to question or accusations of illegality. Owen had done his
duty for the nation this time, but if Arrowsmith came by
again, his answer would probably be no. On the other hand,
four Owen Parcher paintings were now part of the permanent collection at the grand building on Piccadilly.

Sims now had two published novels, and the one still in manuscript that had caused such a rumpled Christmas back in Philadelphia. He wanted a definite change in subject matter for the new work, but still keeping his themes of a man not fitting in with a new environment and trying to go forward against those who made a wall against his progress. Hank's tales of San Ildefonso Pueblo kept coming up in his mind, so much past violence and grief in what now looked like a place of simplicity and peace. Was it too foreign a subject, too apart from his own experience for him to tell? Could an Anglo author truly tell a story of a native culture?

The more he thought about it and made notes for possible chapters, he knew that any saga of a young man fighting against a staid older generation was universal. Change probably happened more slowly in a pueblo than in the world outside, but the visual memory of the power pole behind Hank's family earthen house said that change did occur. First there was a light bulb in the main room, then a small electric heater, the General Electric refrigerator would have been a great leap forward, and maybe in the future a round-screen television. They were only slow steps, the thin edges of wedges growing wider, but change had in fact occurred.

Thinking of Aunt Clara, still unmarried, living with her mother, Sims wondered if he could switch genders in his choice of narrator, make Clara the one who strived to establish her own identity, different from the staid ways of the pueblo? Perhaps her pots were the way out from under the heavy yoke of family. How could that be? Could a unique glaze or design make the difference so that she could break free? How exactly would breaking free show itself in a pueblo culture? Was that part of why she was still unmarried? Could there be a chance of marriage in the future, and what sort of man would that be?

Soon it became clear that an Aunt Clara character *was* the answer. She had lived through the fighting between kivas that Hank talked about, seen a pueblo divided and the experience of deciding there was more than one way forward. Change became a byword for Clara. She would have been twenty years old during the recent war years and the great activity at nearby Los Alamos. There surely was a possibility for some sort of employment or mission there in the Manhattan Project for a young Pueblo woman.

That evening Sims asked, "Hank, would there be something wrong in my basing the main character of a novel on your Aunt Clara?"

"I don't know. Probably not."

"I would change the people's names, but keep the pueblo name. San Ildefonso has such a ring to it. A coming of age in the pueblo, making sense of a threatening modern world."

"We should go out and ask her," Hank said.

"Could I go, too?" Owen asked. "I have some ideas for Black Mesa paintings."

The next day they drove north, Owen with his sketchbook and stool, and Sims with a notebook with lined pages.

As they passed the mesa, they left Owen to sit in the shade of a spreading Russian olive tree with his folding stool. Sims and Hank went on to the pueblo.

Clara opened the door before they knocked. Hank had made many trips out to the pueblo since their last visit, but this was the first return for Sims. Clara looked the same as before, not appreciably older. Hank spoke in Tewa to her for a minute or two. She showed no reaction on her face, looking at times over to Sims.

She smiled shyly as Sims gave her an inscribed copy of *The Uttermost Parts of the Sea.* As before, they went into the back garden. The grandmother was nowhere to be seen, in the house or in the garden, but Clara brought out the orange sodas and pies, a necessary beginning to any pueblo get-together. She remembered that Sims on his first visit had asked to see her pots, so they went around to an adjoining house, her pottery studio, to see her work. Clara said that this was the room where she showed her pots to collectors who came to the pueblo, now several last month all the way from Germany. She actually crafted the pots in the adjoining room.

The wooden shelves in the first room held her pots in a single row. Sims knew that the iconic pots of the pueblo were finely polished black and matte black, but Clara's were quite different. Hank related that Clara and her cousins walked up to the top of Black Mesa as children, picking up the broken shards of pots along the way. She loved the many colors she saw in them, the old colors from Rio Grande clays, unlike the unrelenting dark black product of the most famous of pueblo potters. While the world's collectors knew Maria Martinez's pots for their fine, shiny black surfaces, there was a smaller group of collectors who thought Clara's ochre, white, and charcoal gray pots the finest of them all. Most of hers were simple ollas, but there were also marriage pots with their inward curving tops and straight-sided canisters, a more modern shape.

The designs on her pots were abstracted shapes from nature, branches, leaves, clouds, lightning, rain, but no animals. One pot had very thin black lines on a white ground around the whole pot, undulating here and there like a rainstorm in the wind. There were oval shapes in the rain containing ochre leaves that had blown up in the wind. The land below was a simple band of a darker shade of ochre. There were other versions with ochre rain lines on a black background, with a white band below — variations on a theme. These were modern pots, Sims thought, quite beyond the inherited patterns from early times. He would not ask the question, but wondered how the other pueblo potters regarded Clara's work. Was there a sharp rivalry between the women? Was using a new design like a heresy against the others? If all seemed calm and friendly in the present-day pueblo, the years of conflict between the kivas said otherwise. Clara had fought many battles to do her different work, he was sure. There was a story here.

Sims could picture in his mind the through-line for his book. He liked that it was a woman's tale, but knew it would be harder for him to write. Finding the way to do it would be a challenge, perhaps studying closer the work of Virginia Woolf and Pearl Buck. And maybe there would be some hints in Jane Austen. It was going to be an interesting year. He did not want to write in the manner of a woman, but in the manner of a man who could hear the story of a woman, tell it to others. He knew there was a difference between the two.

"I will read your book, Sims," Clara said. "But mine is a much simpler story, I am sure."

"I don't know that," Sims answered. "It will not be a biography, Clara, but a work of fiction about a woman like you. There will be a struggle, and I like stories with both danger and joy, so it will not be a peaceful story. May I show you the first draft?"

"Please."

"Perhaps in the fall."

They left with a stack of Clara's prune pies wrapped in wax paper, as well as a warm, round loaf of pueblo bread that no visitor left without. Sims wondered if the German collectors took their loaves all the way back to the fatherland to eat a slice with Munster cheese and a cold beer, a talisman of their adventures abroad.

While Sims absorbed the human motifs for his book, Owen had filled a sketchbook with stony drawings of the mesa when they picked him up from the roadside. He showed Sims and Hank his black-inked pages before they started up again. They were not realistic renditions of the Black Mesa's shape, but lines that tumbled down across the page, divided and rejoined the way the volcanic sides of the mesa did. Owen also included detailed drawings of the straight up-and-down cliff-sides and others with the patterns of the way rocks were strewn about the base. There were also drawings of the particular way the talus slope came out from the vertical cliffs, a geologic angle that you could immediately recognize, the angle of repose. At least a dozen pages delineated the way the clusters of piñon evergreens got thinner and thinner as they went up the slopes, vegetation struggling as it got drier and more volcanic.

It had been a rewarding trip up to San Ildefonso, Sims

thought, both he and Owen collecting inspirations like shards from the ground, each with a pocketful. Should they feel guilty at robbing this private land of ideas, as if they were actual shards? A painter friend of theirs told the story of setting up his easel *plein-air* to paint the West Mesa on the side of the highway that went through the San Ildefonso pueblo lands. After an hour or so the pueblo police stopped by, saying he could not paint their pueblo without permission. Only the cacique could give that permission, and he would not be available until the middle of next week. The bounty of pueblo lands was not there for anyone and everyone, even the images must be held close to the chest.

DINNER PLANS

The busy stream of customers around Friday midday had slowed down almost entirely, so Viona decided to close the shop early. It was early enough to meet Hank at La Fonda bar for a drink, before the late afternoon crush began. Hank had stayed a steady friend throughout the years, and he was now her personal attorney, as well. He was already at the bar. They kissed and she sat down next to him.

"Busy week?" he asked.

"Sales are good."

"What did you want to talk to me about?"

"Let me get a drink first. Vermouth and soda, please."

Viona told Hank about Martin, the man she had met after Sophia de la Peña left for Mexico. He kept asking her to marry, not sharp and insistent about it, but also never giving up. Martin was handsome, kind, and apparently rich. It should be an easy decision, but Viona said she was not sure she should be with a man. She enjoyed sex with a man, but there had been a deeper attraction, a more satisfying love with a woman. Especially with Sophia. Not making the decision keep her up at night.

"Maybe you should just wait," Hank said.

"I know. I wonder why I can't decide on one person, when you found two."

"It was easy for me."

"There must be problems, jealousy sometimes?"

"There are, but not jealousy."

"What then?"

"We talk about our threesome all the time. Owen and Sims want it to be as equals, like a triangle, Owens says. It is new to them, too."

"I don't understand."

"I love each of them equally, they love me equally. We are all the exact same distance apart."

"Does it work?"

"We always wait until all three of us can get together in bed."

"What do three men do in bed?"

Hank thought how difficult it was to put their love into words. There were encounters before Sims and Owen came to town, sometimes just a one-night stand and several going for a number of weeks. Gilbert knew what had happened on the nights when Hank was late, but he never found fault with Hank. He made a time to tell Hank, almost out of the blue as they were working at the station, how sorry he was that he himself had never found love and how important it was for a young person to find it. There would be no possibilities in later age. It was as close as he came to outright approval.

"I'll try to tell you without being too crude. Owen and Sims loved each other totally before me, and now I am the one they chose to be between them. On some nights I face Owen and others I face Sims. They love each other through me."

"Do you ever change that?"

"Sometimes, but that is what we all liked the best right from the beginning."

"Okay, I won't press you any further."

"Viona, it's not that I want to hide anything. I just don't have the words to describe how it is, how great it is. How lucky we all are."

"Do you think they feel that way?"

"We talk about it, so I know they do. I do wonder, though, if people are always trying to have that first night of love again? And again."

"I can't imagine being with two women. Or, for that matter, two men. Or now that I think about it, even one."

"You don't have to. Do you want to join us up at Summerville for dinner?"

"Let me get us another drink. Martin is taking me to dinner, later."

"Maybe tonight, the answer."

"And maybe not."

TO HAVE A HANDSOME FATHER

I'll come get you, Papa," Owen said.

He was talking on the telephone to Isaac in the big house in Philadelphia, quiet as never before now that Augustine had died of a failed heart. The funeral was over a month ago, the staff finally taking down the black wreaths on all the doors. Owen, still worried about the depressed state of his father, returned to Santa Fe and continued his work at the easel. He knew that Isaac now must come to live with them at Summerville House, it was the only solution. Isaac needed time to see the wisdom of this and that time had passed.

Owen told his father he would drive the Packard convertible to the East Coast and bring him back to Santa Fe. There were empty houses in the compound and he would ask Perfecto and Rita to get one ready for a new, long-term resident. The drive back would give them time to talk, to mend the unhappy passages of the last few years.

"You're a good son, Owen. I'll be ready."

"There is only a small luggage compartment, so pack lightly. We'll outfit you here with new togs for the West."

"May I get a black ten-gallon hat?"

"And there's a man here who makes the finest boots."

"Owen, you know your mother loved you."

"I know, Papa."

"She came from an earlier world, could not understand."

"I have forgiven."

"Good. We can start to recover."

"I'm looking forward to it, Papa. You'll love it here in Santa Fe, I know."

Owen drove the five days to Philadelphia and five days back with his father. They took turns at the wheel of the Packard, which operated without a problem the whole way. Isaac had in the Philadelphia garage a Forest Green 1938 Packard four-door sedan with a winged hood ornament and Lalique lights, and it was still admired by passersby, but the canary yellow, convertible two-seater was another experience entirely, a symbol of escape to the sunny uplands. The sedan, on the other hand, was an emblem of the backward-looking world they were leaving behind.

The Parcher house butler and cook would stay on, look after the valuable house, start the sedan engines of the Packard and other cars on a weekly basis, keeping everything ready for a return. Theodore, who had waited on the sidelines for this era to start, was already ensconced at Parcher headquarters by the river, planning for the growth and expansion that had always eluded Isaac. House and business would be in safe hands, and it was clear to Owen that the move west was only on a trial basis.

On their second day, driving through eastern Tennessee, Isaac was at the wheel.

Owen noticed that Isaac was bolder in his talk while driving, quicker to bring up the many issues between them. Maybe there were magic powers of truth coursing up his arms when his hands clasped the Packard's pear-wood steering wheel.

"Son, Sims's first manuscript caused much unhappiness a few years ago. Augustine read it in one sitting and couldn't stop talking about it. She hated that you and Sims were admitted homosexuals."

"It was a novel, Papa."

"But we saw through to the real story."

"You're right. Sims and I were lovers even before we went into the Army. Those summers back on the farm, we discovered each other."

"We never knew. What do you think causes it?"

"Papa, we just come that way. We don't decide to become gay, it's just there."

"Augustine thought it might have been her fault."

"No, but it is surely hereditary, like blue eyes. Let's look at the family. Your mother had maiden aunts that never married and Uncle Theodore is definitely gay, but he has successfully hidden it all from you, not dropped any hairpins, as they say. It's just in the family."

"It's true, we all looked the other way about Theodore. He is now such an accomplished executive, probably always was, even though we held him back. Actually, I also had a short homosexual experience at university. Nothing came of it, of course. I met your mother and thought that life with her was the only way. A man needed to marry in my time."

"I knew that. I'm glad times are different now."

"What of Sims's manuscript? Will it be published eventually?"

"You'll have to ask him."

Owen thought about how handsome his father still was and wondered about the extent of his adventures down that other pathway at university. He certainly would have had other opportunities. Owen was convinced that Isaac could have had more than his one experience. And just how short was his one professed experience? A week or a couple of years? Could memories of that first love still wing their way through Isaac's dreams today, a wisp of what could have been but could never be mentioned? Was it the first love, or just the one he chose to disclose?

As difficult as it had been for Sims and Owen, and now Hank, to be open and honest, he knew it was all but impossible for Isaac not to marry and put the questions to rest. Isaac, the industrialist's elder son, was a toothsome catch for one of the plain but rich Fairfax sisters back in the 1920s, and the quick production of a son quelled any unsavory questions. The next day, driving through Arkansas with Isaac as a passenger and Owen at the wheel, they talked about more of the other unmarried uncles and cousins in the family.

"What about Mother's brother and sister who never married, but lived out on the farm together?" Owen asked. "Don't you think they were gay, afraid to get married to others, hiding in the country?"

"Not at all. Your mother said incest was their problem, not homosexuality."

"And that was somehow okay, but horrors if there was a gay son?"

"There's no logic to it."

"Well, sometime in the future it will make no matter."

"Son, I will try to make it no matter right now. I should have long ago."

"Thanks, Papa."

"I should tell you something Augustine said before she went. She asked me how it was that you and Sims seemed to be the happiest couple, more in love than the whole rest of the family. Almost the best marriage."

"I wish she had told me herself."

"If she had more time, she would have, son. She was coming around. I told her that we should be proud of our very own Achilles and Patroclus."

"What did she say to that?"

"Your mother never heard me when I talked about the Greeks. Ear lids closed."

"Well, I hope our future is better than Achilles and Patroclus, despite their happy times."

"The other thing Augustine worried about was that you would not stay together all your lives, as a properly married couple."

"Like you and Mother, Papa?"

"Touché."

"And you haven't met our Hank Garcia. He's become very important to Sims and me."

"I am not sure I understand."

"You will."

The five days of being together had proved their worth for father and son. If they felt they had been reasonably close before, closer certainly than mother and son, the bond was much stronger now. Owen was driving as they came into Santa Fe, giving Isaac a running commentary on the parts of the town. As Owen paused the car at the gate as he had years before, Isaac's eyes got moist. He could not help thinking about Ithaca, Odysseus home again with his son.

Perfecto and Rita worked wonders with the cottage, which had not been used since the Chinese mathematics teacher was there fifteen years ago. It needed a thorough cleaning out, opened up for the breezes to sweep away the musty air, fabrics aired in the sun, new paint on the walls, wax on the dark brick floors, and, thanks to Rita, a bowl of lavender stalks to scent the air. The mathematics teacher's protractor, slide rule, compass, pencils with red erasers, and book of trigonometry tables were all gathered together in a basket on the side table. It was dark and cool inside the house, Owen leaving Isaac to take a nap before meeting all the others at dinner. The Packard convertible's windshields and radiator cover desperately needed attention, the smashed insects and butterflies waiting to be scraped and washed away, its automotive style and authority restored.

SOME OOLONG

S ims searched for and found a daybed in one of the Summerville cottages and added it to his spare writing cottage. He had read that the novelist Anthony Powell thought
out his involved plots lying down on a daybed, saying that
he could tap into another part of his brain, the one that knew
the answers when he was prone for an hour or two. In the
writing of the pueblo story, the daybed proved to be a valuable tool. It must not be a mere sofa, Sims decided, but
a true daybed with the spirit of Powell floating overhead.
From the first pages, the tale of the pueblo potter and her
slow-paced war against the forces of imbedded custom felt
right. She fought differently from a man and that was what
came up when Sims lay down, letting the gates of invention
open in his mind.

He asked Hank to take him back to talk to Clara, knowing it probably was not proper for him to interview without
a family member as a chaperone. Clara was diffident about
talking about herself, but more open in lore of the pueblo
itself. She gave them a tour of the plaza and the common
fields beyond, the paths to Black Mesa, the river and the
West Mesa. They peered into the windows of the vacant hall
where the council met and into the pottery studio of another
woman potter. She said the tradition of watching a potter at

work was strong at San Ildefonso, but no actual teaching of their methods was encouraged. Young potters, in silence, watched the movements of the older potters.

Sims read Robert Graves's Greek Myths, particularly the legends of the female gods. While Greek women were strong, always on alert to the mischief from the other gender, Sims was mostly on his own with this story. He let his imagination lead him on details of a young girl's life, her friends and what they did. The all-girl boarding school away from the pueblo would not have been a great deal different from his own all-boy version, friends and foes in teacup tempests, teachers who opened vistas and those that shut them down, too seldom going for vacations back home, sporting times on grass or dirt fields, and the myriad childhood worries of not fitting in as well as the others. If she survived it, as he had, it gave strength for what was to come.

His narrator might well have had a cousin as close as Owen had been to him, a young woman, or young man, who understood it all without words. He decided it would not be as sexual a pairing as Owen and he had, but he did not want to avoid hints of such attraction. The characters grew in number, good and bad, some verging on evil itself. Rewarding episodes were followed by thwarting ones as the girl became a woman. Her determination in life was set into the bones early and gave her the strength to go down the different artistic path, where there was nobody to encourage her. And, near the end of his book, Sims felt he was at one with her voice and knew she was rewarded in the very act of making art.

Hank read the first draft, correcting mistakes Sims made in the workings of the pueblo. Sims told Hank that it was not to be viewed as a monograph on the history of Pueblo people, but a simple story of woman who just happened to be part of a native community. She was battling the phalanx of elders who did not want change, finding a dance, a way to still live in their midst. It could as well have been the story of an Anglo girl from a fundamentalist Midwest town or a highborn story of a girl fighting against the society matrons of the Mainline. Sims's Clara character would have to tread carefully and not fail to attend the ceremonies and dances, but in quiet determination strike out on her own in the lesser world of pottery.

Hank asked Sims to read out loud the book to Clara rather than just let her have it. The three of them sat in her pottery house while he read, most of a long afternoon. Clara smiled and nodded to Hank when Sims finished. They talked back and forth in Tewa, and she came over to kiss Sims on the forehead. They left with another loaf of pueblo bread in a brown paper bag.

Typing up the revised manuscript, Sims thought that maybe Prestor might not be the only meaningful advisor on this work. He had two typewritten copies, the original and a carbon, to parcel out. Of course, he would give Prestor a copy, and he wondered if Mary Louise Aston was in Santa Fe on one of her now longer and longer visits to Agnes Tibbs. He called the Tibbs number.

"Mary Louise here."

"Oh, I'm so glad to reach you."

"What news?"

"I have a manuscript I would love for you to read. Is that possible?"

"Perfectly. Bring it over right now."

On the way over to the Tibbs studio, he left the carbon

copy in Prestor McCain's mail box. There was actually a compound of houses at the Tibbs address, similar to Summerville School but not so large. At the far back, away from Canyon Road, Mary Louise was waiting at the Dutch door of a house beside which was the small sign, Long House.

"I've made some Oolong. Come in and sit."

"I really appreciate this."

"You were right about your summer camp stories, they did not work for my magazine. But they were well-written with interesting characters. Did you place them elsewhere?"

"No, they are still in my desk drawer. I thought you might be interested in my story of a woman who also happens to be a potter. A new novel, but shorter than the others."

"I have an open afternoon. I'll call you tomorrow."

They talked for a while about other matters, what was happening in the New York world of books. Mary Louise said that Jacob Bourne and his lover were to visit them for Thanksgiving, and did Sims's "tribe" want to join them for the meal? There would be others as well. *Literary and artistic lions*, she said, *growling over turkey and dressing.*

Sims told Hank and Owen that night what he had done with his manuscripts. Owen was just about finished with his series of Black Mesa paintings, these smaller than his usual six-by-six panels. Hank had just been chosen as a legal advisor for another northern pueblo, his expertise in tribal affairs being recognized.

"We mustn't be too smug. But it is a fine harvest for all of us, and that doesn't happen very often to us at the same time," Sims said.

"A special toast, then. Without hubris," Owen replied.

Sims worried that he would not sleep well with his new pages being judged and perhaps found lacking. Owen usually turned new paintings to the wall for a week or two, then turned them around to make a judgment. Perhaps he should have waited with the manuscript, set it in the bottom drawer and reread it after a suitable time. It was done, now. So he would do his usually successful maneuver to bring on sleep, shut his eyes and focus his mind-eyes on a long blue line until darkness crept its way in by inches from either side.

STUBBY CLUMPS OF IRIS

Although the twosome of Sims and Owen had been around for much longer, Sims realized that this was nearing the tenth year of their threesome. He knew that their life at the secluded Summerville House was similar to monastic life, single males walled away from most of the community with only the occasional interaction with their neighbors. It only lacked the monastery bells to call them to work and, later, to gather back in the house. The town certainly knew of their existence, but there were many other artists and writers in Santa Fe who chose to be very private, so Summerville House was not all that unusual. Artists were respected and treasured, allowed to exist in the apartness, but their oddness was a continual topic of town conversations.

Sims, more than the other two, thought about such things as their vulnerability to malicious gossip and accusatory stories. The laws were not on their side, even though the town looked the other way when it came to their treasured artists. There was an incident waiting to happen, Sims thought, sooner or later.

He had been thinking about these very matters when there was a knock on the door to his writing cottage. It was Hank's brother, Adam, whom he had met only several times during these years.

"Hello, Adam. What brings you here?"

"We better go inside."

"Sit down over there."

"Hank's all right, I guess?"

"You should go to his law office and ask him."

Sims saw that Adam had his brother's good looks, but in an unfortunate form. His face was longer than Hank's square one, but the eyes and eyebrows were the same.

He was taller than Hank, not so much a man of the ground. Sims noticed he had small hands, not the square big ones he knew so well.

"I'll get right to it. You know sodomy is a crime in New Mexico. I looked it up, a fine of a thousand dollars and up to fifteen years in the slammer."

"So?"

"I need money to go to California, get away from this queer town. My house is mortgaged to the hilt and I don't have a bank account, like you rich boys."

The purpose of Adam's visit became clear to Sims. Adam would ask for some amount of money or he would go public about the threesome. Sims wondered if he would actually put this into words.

"What do you want, Adam?"

"I will go to the police and accuse Hank of raping me when we were boys. They will say I should have done that years ago, please go away. Statute of limitations. But the papers will pick up on it, I will make sure of it. Lawyer Accused By Brother of Sodomy Rape. Hank's law business will go away. Nobody will come to your smart parties anymore."

"Unless..."

"Five thousand dollars."

"Get out, Adam. It's nothing but blackmail," Sims said, standing up from his desk.

"I'll wait a week," he said, keeping his eye on Sims as he walked to the door. Sims watched him going down the pathway from the door, Adam looking back now and then.

Sims knew that this would hurt Hank very much, but he had to tell him. He waited until after dinner, when Rita had left the kitchen and gone home, before speaking up. He told the story slowly to Owen and Hank.

"You know," said Hank, "it was the other way around. Adam raped me when we were in our early teens. He called me a fruit boy. That's when I decided to work out and get stronger, learn how to wrestle, so nobody else could do that to me. Took some boxing lessons, too."

"I'm so sorry, Hank," Owen said. "Even though it is not right, Sims and I can certainly pay him off, let him go out of town."

"I stayed away from him until after I was strong enough, big enough to fight back. He never did it again and I could see he became afraid to try."

"I will ask if he will take three thousand," Owen said.

"Let me handle Adam, Owen," Hank said. "My brother is a bad seed, but I am not afraid of him anymore."

"We should go with you."

"No, I need to do this by myself."

Hank went by the family house on Manhattan Street the next afternoon, after going to his office to make some phone calls. As he walked up the front walk, he remembered his mother's flower garden in the front, behind the high wall on the street. She and his father built the adobe wall together, finished it with mud plaster, the garden a private place to remind her of her pueblo home. Now the garden was bare dirt, only stubby clumps of iris foliage, choked with weeds, in the dry beds. His mother's beloved apricot tree, a seedling dug up and moved from the pueblo, was barely alive, branches covered with lace vine. He knocked on the door.

"My pansy-ass brother," Adam said.

"Let's sit down, Adam. I'm happy you are going to California. We should be brothers, but we aren't. Sims and Owen are more my brothers than you."

"Not brothers, a bunch of perverts."

"Here's my one and only offer. You will sign the deed to the house to me for five thousand dollars. I will take over the mortgage on the house, get it up to date. You will get out of town by the end of the week."

"It's worth a lot more than five thousand," Adam said, moving forward as if to do harm, then thinking about it and moving back.

"Not if the bank repossesses it on the mortgage. Victor Romero at the bank said they are going to do that by the end of the month because of your nonpayment on installments."

"So you've spied on me."

"You only got the mortgage *because* of Victor, dad's cousin. He said he's ready to give up on you. Bad mistake, he told me."

"It's a smelly house, anyway. Dead mice under the floor."

"I will have the cash for you tomorrow, if you agree to leave now."

"Some way to treat a brother."

"I wish we *were* brothers, Adam."

"How about six thousand?"

"All right."

A few weeks after their deal had transacted, Hank heard

stories that Adam did not go directly to California, but moved in with a girlfriend. She reported a domestic disturbance to the police a couple of weeks later, but Adam was nowhere to be found. Hank felt that this was not the true end of the matter, that brother Adam would turn up again.

BLACK BEETLE

Mary Louise's living room was long, with a multi-sashed window at its end, walls hung with the earthen-colored, petroglyph hangings of Agnes Tibbs, the dining table with a white cloth. It was Mary Louise's Thanksgiving spread, with a name card at each plate, the hostess thinking out in advance who might converse well with whom, a matter she never left to chance. Guests took their plates to the buffet table in the adjoining kitchen and returned loaded with the festive fare. The preceding cocktail hour let loose the decibel level of the conversations about art and writing, a little about gardening, but no current events welcomed.

Mary Louise seated Prestor McCain to her right and Sims to her left, obviously wanting to talk books with her turkey slices. At first there was holiday talk all around the table, when the first flakes of the expected snowstorm would arrive and who else was in town from New York. Prestor was the first to get to the matter of Sims's pueblo book, now in finish production at the Small and Redd printers. Everyone who mattered had already read the publisher's advance copies, writing blurbs and reviews, so Sims's *From the Earth Itself* was fair game as a subject.

"Sims, my dear boy," Prestor said, "the third book of

most novelists is almost always a disappointment and yours is no exception. Don't despair, you are in the company of the very best. The writer needs to expunge this third book, get it out of his system, before going on to more worthwhile attempts. If I cannot heap praise on this story, I know that an admirable fourth novel is already under way."

Sims wondered if his giving the carbon copy of the manuscript to Prestor was now coming back to haunt him. Book people, as well as other people, are jealous of their exclusive inside position with authors.

"I don't agree, Prestor," Mary Louise said. "Sims's new book is a capable work, in line with his others. Not a disappointment. Men writers with a female narrator are asking for trouble, however, a specialty reserved for women novelists themselves. We are an ungenerous lot. Sims was brave to try, and succeeded, by and large."

"My next story has a male narrator, once again," Sims said. "I feel more comfortable with that." He was hearing such comments as Prestor's and Mary Louise's from other sources as well. It was as if he had unknowingly walked into the women's side of public baths in writing his story about a potter, the watery women now screaming abuse while they scurried for towels. He was satisfied with what he had written, but there would be no further female voices leading the way in his future books. Sims was learning the necessity of thickening his skin against the javelins that always brushed by the artist who puts something different in front of the public. And, as a novelist, he needed women on his side, not against him.

"I have heard word of many good reviews, however," Mary Louise said. "I would expect the book clubs will be calling you."

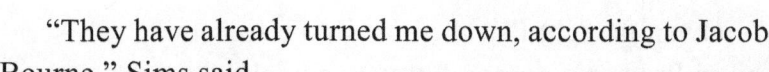

"They have already turned me down, according to Jacob Bourne," Sims said.

"And I am sorry Jordan's did not do the serial I suggested," Mary Louise said. "Your chapters in themselves almost work as short stories, but Carmel Sleet said no."

Parthon Ellis, at the other end of the table, was heaping praise on Owen's new paintings. Owen had given him the day before a private studio showing of the Black Mesa canvases. Parthon was describing them to the others at his end of the table.

"There are ten of them the same size. In shades of black, some warm and others cool. Strong designs, all lines from top to bottom, interspersed with bravura smaller passages of the finest of oil painting. You could almost belong to the Transcendentalist Group in Santa Fe, artists who did not want to paint any more Indians."

"I admire the Transcendentalists, Parthon," Owen said. "Raymond Jonson's work, particularly, seems to be the way forward."

"I'm not so sure that art is a roadway."

"Well, a view of what is to come."

"I hope not entirely. But let's get back to you."

He went on to describe Owen's use of a palette knife in some areas, thick areas of polished paint relieved by portions of matte, a quiet reference to the pottery of the area. He thought he saw some golden sections here and there, the art of Greek proportions taken up as the painter's own. And at length, he recognized Owen's brush stokes in the ten paintings as all related in their dimensions, a rectangle of one on the short side and seven on the long side, again and again. Perhaps the painter was touching upon the little-known rules from the ancient classics.

Owen thought that there might be something self-serving in Parthon's paean of praise, a finely observed account that said Parthon's splendid eye saw remarkable things of which even the painter himself might be unaware. Debate teams must have a Latin term for that type of praise, a glittery coating of sugar over the black beetle of disapproval.

Agnes Tibbs sat at the far end of the long table, looking solid and patriarchal while listening to Parthon's diatribe. In the middle of the table, the Englishwoman Rosalind Sotheby was expounding on what she had seen in New York galleries the week before, exciting dribbles of paint on white panels. A woman painter who sat across from her described afterwards her own exhibit of Mexican street scenes in a downtown Santa Fe gallery. The shy poet Hamish McCloud sat next to her, listening intently but looking down as he picked away on a plate with little meat and dressing, but a pile of cranberry sauce. Viona Maes sat next to him, talking across the table to a woman wearing one of her dresses. Owen winked across at Viona. Sims looked over at the socially uncomfortable Hank sitting next to Prestor, happy to see him talking with hand gestures to the woman painter on his other side, who smiled broadly.

Mary Louise had kindly included Isaac Parcher in her invitation, he sitting next to the woman wearing Viona's dress. Owen observed that Isaac was talking animatedly to the middle-aged woman in Viona's dress, a woman he would understand, and he found a quick moment of silence to pat his father on the back. If there was an Art Central in Santa Fe, Mary Louise's dining table sat on its very center. The table could seat ten in comfort, and twelve or even the sixteen like this festive occasion, with close, bumping elbows, all sitting in mismatched, creaking chairs. Sims wondered how it was that everybody was talking at once, no-body listening. Did the close bumping of elbows bring forth such birdsong, like a row of finches along a tree branch?

"Tell me, Sims, about this fourth novel," Mary Louise said, with Prestor listening in.

"With the same male narrator as the first book, I'm going back to London during the Blitz. A light-hearted sort of spy story. Owen and I were there, and I have been mining the journal that I kept for details. It's how a man finds happiness in such a maelstrom."

"You might want to talk with Rosalind. She was there in the Red Cross."

"Such a tense time," Prestor said. "I was in New York during the war. There was talk of Nazi submarines off Long Island, but no buzz bombs actually falling on the next street like you, Sims."

"Your light-hearted spy story sounds very intriguing," Mary Louise said. "Men usually like spies better than women do, however."

"I think women will also like this one," Sims said.

"Then, what about a light-hearted spy short story for me? We'll try with the particular Mrs. Sleet once again."

The dinner party ended after dark. In the falling snow, Owen, Sims, Hank, and Isaac walked back up Canyon Road with a flashlight and over to Summerville House. They could see the tracks of a rabbit across the snowy soccer field as they headed for the front door, the lights from inside the house making long yellow rectangles out and across the snow.

OLD CRABAPPLE TREES

Isaac Parcher was a walker, getting up early at his Summerville cottage and taking a different way each day down to the central Plaza in Santa Fe. Native American men would be clearing off the museum portal with sweeps of their blankets, brooms being non-masculine and beneath them, and definitely not so dramatic as the swirling of a black-and-white striped blanket. The jewelry market would be set up thereafter on the clean pavement of the portal. Merchants were opening their stores, washing their plaza-side windows with squeegees, and the smell of coffee from the drugstore wafted across the grass. Isaac often sat for a while on one of the cast-iron plaza benches. It was a good time to ponder the past while watching the world of plaza commerce re-emerge for the day.

He thought there about his Augustine, how uncomfortable she would have been in Santa Fe. There were so many aspects to the town that now pleased him he knew she would find tiresome and tawdry. The informality of dress, the spicy menus, dinner parties on unmatching, rickety chairs, the desultory clearing of plates, guest lists that included a cross-section of social strata, Anglo women in Navajo dress, silver jewelry itself, streets without sidewalks, houses made from mud instead of stone and all the rest. She was a died-in-the-wool city person. What Isaac had always admired about Augustine was her great sense of urban style, wearing hats that nobody else could wear and dresses that made other women turn their heads. She was happiest in the keen competition of Philadelphia society, a place she knew that she was an able and successful participant, winning a new, minor battle every week. Santa Fe would have been a horrid, unknown place for her, a different brazenry to confront every day. He had loved Augustine and given her the wide berth she needed, taking her side in the dinnertime recounting of the social skirmishes that filled her days.

She did not die quickly, but in slow steps down over several months. Isaac thought the two of them were closer during those months than at any time during their marriage. Augustine forbade Isaac from informing Owen of her condition, seeing mostly Isaac and the housemaids as her strength waned. Her sister Isabel came by every day, but few others.

"Isaac, you must remarry quickly," she said towards the end.

"I probably won't," he answered.

"This is a big house to be all alone in. There are several suitable widows nearby."

"I know, dear."

"You might just make a visit out west to Owen, afterward."

"I'll wait until he asks."

Most of their life together, Augustine had read novels on her side of the bed before they went to sleep, so Isaac starting reading aloud to her each evening, John O'Hara, Somerset Maugham, Evelyn Waugh and both of Sims's novels. She complimented Isaac's speaking voice, wondering why they had not done this in their earlier, healthier years.

"Sims has become a good writer," she said after Isaac concluded his first novel.

"We are lucky to have such a nephew."

"I suppose I was wrong about the safe-deposit manuscript."

"You felt strongly, never a bad thing."

"Owen and Sims have made a good life together. I should be happy."

"I still don't know how it happened."

"Tell Sims I *am* sorry. After I'm gone. I don't want a kerfuffle now."

Shortly after this exchange, Augustine fell into a coma, the end a few days after that. She would have appreciated the funeral itself, a large Philadelphia crowd in fashionable black for the Anglican service, as well as at the graveside, the old crabapple trees between the family plots in full blossom and a still, sunny afternoon. And there were many, new black hats on the women, purchased especially for the occasion.

Owen came for the funeral and stayed on with Isaac for a few days at the house, in his old room. Isaac remembered the echoes bouncing around in the house in the days afterwards, echoes he had never heard before. He wondered if he would adjust to this new life alone in the big house, Owen promising to come East often.

Those memories of the echoes were fading, he thought as he sat on the plaza. A woman he had seen several times before on the plaza stopped to say hello. He invited her to sit down.

"I'm new in town," Isaac said. "Staying with my son."

"I'm new, too. Just rented a small house for a year."

"Are you an artist?"

"No, but I wanted to be in a town full of them. A new life in Bohemia."

"Would you like to meet my son, the painter Owen Parcher?"

"Oh yes, I just saw his paintings at the Halcyon Gallery. The Black Mesa Paintings."

"I'm very proud."

Isaac judged her to be in her late fifties, still fit and trim. She must be a walker, too, as he had seen her downtown several times in the last weeks, even on a morning with light rain. She exuded a fine forceful quality, not unlike Augustine's. Would the two of them have been friends or enemies?

"From here we could go up to his studio tomorrow, about this time?"

"I would love that. A chance to try out my Scottish walkers."

"It's a date."

GEMSTONE STICKPINS

S ummerville House was a long way from the East Coast, and a long way from the commercial and political dramas that lived such an active existence there. One part of the complex life that kept finding its way west was espionage. Peter Arrowsmith did not let loose whatever hold he had on Owen. On the second occasion when he walked onto their front portal, Sims thought back to their days in London during the war — did Owen find the dashing Major Arrowsmith sexually attractive? He continued to be handsome and fit even now. Were there secret meetings between them in the same rooms on the side streets of St. James that Owen had found so quickly for the two of them? Just like the fog, London was covered over with secrecy, and now even more hidden in the passage of time. It was much too late for jealousy to raise its head, he knew.

This second time Colonel Arrowsmith arrived without an announcement beforehand, Owen asked Sims and Hank to stay and hear what was proposed. Arrowsmith said that he and Owen would pose as father and son on a trip to Beirut, Lebanon. Information would be posted in the correct places that they owned a large, private investment bank, wanting to expand internationally. Beirut was the money capital of the Middle East, as well as capital of covert arms sales and clandestine contracts of all sorts.

In the cocktail lounges of the better hotels, they would put out the word that there was a massive amount of private capital available for other, important bankers and their projects. The rest of the mission was classified. It would only take a trip of a week to make a catch, and Owen had the looks and patrician bearing to be unquestioned as a banker's son. There were no ways to fake such things, Owen being the perfect and only one for the ruse, his top-secret clearance still in place. It was the equitable way he looked at other people, Arrowsmith said, that told everything. Sims wanted to delve deeper into this cover story.

"Are you married, Colonel Arrowsmith?" Sims asked.

"Divorced now, for the last ten years."

"We are very defensive of our Owen, you know."

"As you should be."

"There must be danger involved."

"Not really. Only subterfuge, and a touch of counterintelligence."

"All too classified for mere civilians to know?"

"I'm afraid, yes."

"And, of course, this is all for the good of the nation?"

"Absolutely."

"What if Owen just says no?"

"I hope he won't."

With an overnight of thinking and deciding, Owen said yes and went away for a week in the Levant with Arrowsmith, bringing back some large, gemstone stickpins for Hank, Sims, and Isaac, expensive French scarves for Viona and Rita, and a raging head cold. He had very little to say about what happened in Beirut, only that it brought a satisfactory outcome. He did tell of night swimming in the

Mediterranean, a fine, sandy beach in front of their hotel with a luminescence in the warm water.

Sims did not try to question him further. He knew, however, that Arrowsmith had some sort of claim on their Owen, perhaps a secret knowledge of wartime nights when everyone wondered if they would survive the week. Nights in those same St. James rooms, when searchlights scanned the night skies. If he delved deeper, Sims thought he might disclose the information he would be sorry to know. This was the other side of Owen's moon, the side that never turned towards earth. Sims would have to live only with the view towards the sunlit side, while the writer's imagination roiled.

And the world of espionage wandered its way into Sims's life as well. In response to Mary Louise's request, he wrote "a light-hearted spy story" for the women's magazine. It almost wrote itself in the week after Thanksgiving, Mary Louise back in New York. He laughed out loud several times as he plotted the story in his mind while prone on that valuable creative asset, the cottage's daybed, head propped only slightly up, thank you very much Anthony Powell.

The Black Bag of Emily Potts was the story's title, and it started a series of stories with a heroine who carried Bogota rakes and curtain picks in her designer handbag, the classic tools of lock-pickers, and she was quick to purloin necessary documents from the most inner of sanctums, running afterwards high-speed down alleyways in high heels. Emily was on the surface very like a cousin of Sims's, a demure Bryn Mawr graduate, a lithe star of their small track team, but with the added, required talents of trickery, deceit, and the ability to foil even the most German-engineered of locks, while remaining polite and ladylike. There was a back-story of a favorite uncle, somewhat similar to Uncle Theodore, who on the long summer vacations taught his young relative many little-known, mechanical manipulations, the very ones that proved so valuable later in her life. She was an able student, going on her own well past her lessons. Sims pictured in detail Emily's slipping into and out of New York high-rise buildings and minutes later meeting friends on the street-level bar for martinis with the government-toppling documents crumpled into a wad small enough to fit inside her handbag of red Moroccan leather.

The readers of Jordan's Bazaar went crazy. A dozen stories followed and Emily Potts became the independent woman of the 1950s, besting the feckless men agents in their own world. Each successive story brought a larger check from Jordan's, and a note from Mary Louise requesting another Emily story.

Sims asked Small and Redd to put all the stories together into a book. *The Secret World of Emily Potts* sold more copies than any of Sims's other works, and the Association of Women's Magazines sent Sims a golden high-heeled shoe award for the best woman's book of the year. With wistfulness, Sims tried not to be annoyed at such an inconsequential, non-literary honor, and wished it had been given for his serious novels instead.

TWO ROWS OF MARIGOLDS

The small adobe house on Manhattan Street, where Hank grew up with his parents and brother Adam, was in bad shape, but it was now legally his. Hank found a time to go by there every day on his way to his office, just sitting for a while and thinking about what to do with it. It was the first spring after Adam had left town, the apricot tree's few good limbs in enthusiastic bloom. During the winter Hank repaired the inside problems, pulled away the choking vines and trimmed the dead branches of the apricot, trying to start the reversal of Adam's years of neglect. Juniper incense was the remedy, Clara told him, to cleaning out any spirits that might linger, so he burned twigs with the berries and let the smoke fill the house. Even weeks later, the aroma lingered.

Gilbert died and left in his will both his house and gas station to Hank, so he was now by death or departure a substantial property owner. The station was leased out to a cousin and Gilbert's house rented to a young painter, but Hank did not want to share his mother's house. Although it had come from his father's family, the house with the high wall and front garden was always his mother's house.

The gardens were definitely hers, the six apple trees she planted behind the house with native grasses between them and, in her time, the well-tended front garden, behind the high adobe wall. Hank remembered helping her when he was a small boy, weeding with hands far down on an adult-sized hoe between the rows of pinto beans and squashes.

He could hear her voice, *Get all the bind-weed, son, even the roots.*

The brick entry path divided the two parts of the garden, the southern part reserved for rows of corn in the summer, cabbages in the fall and winter. The other side held closely spaced rows of onions, lettuce, radishes, and eggplants, with the occasional lines of marigolds and iris. His mother said that the marigolds protected the other plants, drove away insects. Hank, of course, knew he was romanticizing his past, giving it a golden veneer of paradise where there would have been no insects or hungry raccoons coming over the back fence, or skunks burrowing under it.

Memories came up by themselves every time he walked through the front door of the house, voices in his mind. He thought of the time early on when he and Adam got along without quarrels. What had made Adam so angry? Hank could not recall. Maybe more time spent in the house would clear away the mists, bring up the answers.

At Summerville House, Hank described to the others the project of the front garden. He wanted to restore it and keep it like it had been. He thought it would be a good foil to his inactive hours of law work, physical versus mental. An hour of tending each day before the office would be enough.

"I need the exercise, too," Sims said. "Sitting at my writing desk is not the best for long-term health."

"Well, the whole front garden needs turning over. I have a load of sheep manure already there to dig it in. If you really want to, it's a lot of work."

"I'll pass on the digging," Owen said, "but when you get to the planting, Isaac and I are the best."

"This weekend, then."

Owen relented and took his turn digging and picking the hard soil with the rest of them. By noon the whole garden was turned over. They added the manure, dug that in, and raked both sides of the path smooth. In the following weeks, they sowed the rows of corn and planted small pots and seeds in parallel rows on the other side of the entry path. The neglected iris clumps were dug up, divided, and planted in a single row. Two full rows of marigolds were seeded, just to be sure about the insects. Late frosts held off as if the weather gods approved of this garden. Hank dropped by every morning to water and hoe out the weeds before opening the office downtown. He tried to remember what his mother looked like, but he could only summon up the wide blue stripes of the dress she often wore while in the garden, her face a smooth, blank oval like the Cezanne portraits that they saw in Paris.

As the spring turned to summer, the garden at its fulsome best, Hank wondered what to do with the house itself. He took to the city dump everything that Adam added, leaving only a few chairs and a table from their parents. A rental to a stranger did not seem right, but he thought Auntie Clara could use it as a showplace for her pots in Santa Fe, the pueblo always a difficult, hidden place for collectors to find. Hank checked with the city zoning people and found the house was in an Arts and Crafts zone, perfect for such a use.

Since the publication of *From the Earth Itself*, and the reviews that revealed the true identity of Sims's pueblo protagonist, Clara's pots had become more popular than ever.

Clara found a neighbor living in the pueblo, a young man who could drive into town and open the Manhattan Street house a few days a week. She told Hank that since she never felt at ease in town, it was best for her to stay at home and keep making pots.

It pleased Hank that the house was now used, especially as a continuance of his mother's San Ildefonso people. When he went in the mornings to tend the garden, still driving the now vintage pickup truck, there were often collectors waiting in the shade on the front portal for the house to open.

"Are you the gardener?" a woman asked one day.

"Yes, but only in the mornings."

"Would you consider working in our garden in the afternoons, then?"

THE CORN DANCE

Now that Malvina had celebrated her ninetieth birthday, both the women had lived well past the actuarial tables of the expected age for European females. Malvina walked with a cane, but Alberta remained upright while she walked over to her studio every morning. She was painting for her next show in Paris at the Galerie de Foche and was considered a national treasure by the slow-to-recognize French government. She swam in the pool on the lowest terrace every summer morning, a ceremony involving both Guy Martel to stay beside her down the rough stone steps and the housekeeper, carrying a large towel. Alberta often said the swim was what kept decrepitude at bay and she pushed the swimming season into the cooler days of November, starting again in the often windy days of late March.

Malvina herself never swam, but sometimes accompanied the royal procession down through the terraces of citrus trees. The exact relationship between the two women had changed slowly over the years, the more dominant Malvina ceding power to Alberta in a slow handover. Malvina wondered if Alberta had been the strong one all along, quietly waiting for her time. And there was no question in the minds of all those who visited or worked for the two women who was now the head of household. Malvina remembered her brother Borden talking about what made the good marriage — it was simply where one of the two went out, the other must go in. Now she went in more and Alberta went out more. A matched pair of opposites.

Alberta had not greatly altered her painting style or subjects since that first exhibit in Paris so many years ago. Both Martine and Igor de Foche were now dead, but Martine's son Paul owned and ran the gallery. After a multi-year hiatus while the gallery looked around for younger painters and more cutting-edge work, they returned to certain members of the former painter stable, including Alberta Todd and Leonid Ulensky. Paul de Foche thought it took twenty-five years or more for a trend in art to come back into cycle, so he was enthusiastic about booking Alberta for an exhibit of her now iconic, pueblo-based paintings. Ulensky had abandoned his precisionist portraits and taken up abstraction now that there was no Soviet eye upon what he did.

Unlike most painters whose work got smaller and smaller as they grew older, Alberta's became larger. She now worked on canvases five feet by five feet, ringing for Guy Martel when she needed to turn a panel around or move it off the easel. Instead of the dozens of native dancers in her earlier work, there were now hundreds, great scenes from a viewpoint somewhere in the sky, looking down on the long dancing lines, as if the viewer were a crow flying over the summer day of the Corn Dance.

French gallery-goers now knew what they were looking at, well-painted, contemporary scenes of the first peoples of the American West. The sad history of discrimination and neglect in a nation other than France was a subject dear to the hearts of liberal Paris. Ancient peoples had disappeared from Continental Europe several thousand years ago, but were still alive in the western canyons of America, if only barely.

When you stood back from Alberta's paintings, they could be abstractions of long lines across the canvas in the colors of red earth, sienna, deepest black-green, and ochre. If you came close and looked intently you could see the bells, drums, and flutes in the hands of the dancers, feather headdresses, baskets full of corn on the verges, and the old women with umbrellas on the pueblo roofs, observing the feast day from folding chairs.

Paul de Foche, on his latest trip down to Menton, knocked on her studio door after being directed there by the housekeeper in the main house. "Are you there, Mademoiselle Todd?" he asked.

"Do come in. Paul de Foche, is it?"

"Yes. Is this a convenient time?"

"Of course. Please meet my assistant Guy Martel."

"Charmed," Paul said. "We are so excited about the exhibit."

"You've come to look at the work, I am sure," Alberta said.

"Is that possible?"

"Guy will turn around the canvases. Stacked over there."

Guy put on white gloves before picking up the first painting, leaning it slowly to face out on the adjoining wall. He waited for half a minute in silence, then continued with the next canvas. And he turned around the next, until all eight paintings had been viewed. Each of them was a different view of the same ceremony, some from higher up looking straight down, others from lower down, looking at an angle across the pueblo plaza. There was silence as the three of them looked at the paintings.

"We thought," Paul said, "that we could exhibit the new Ulensky pieces in an adjoining room."

"That would be fine."

"I have the old gallery records of your former prices, but Mademoiselle, what do we think about the price for these?"

"One hundred thousand apiece."

"Euros, I suppose."

"Yes, Euros."

"Very good. Right in l-l-line with Ulensky's new work."

Paul backed out of the door, as if walking away from royalty. Alberta in a flash remembered Igor, and thought she had read somewhere that stammering ran in families, just like curly hair. How sad.

Guy turned the panels around to face the wall once more and Alberta returned to the stool in front of her easel. She thought, what a long curving road it had been to reach this level place. Picasso and Matisse received much more for their paintings, but this was an enormous rise for her. Malvina would be so pleased when she described the interview later today, over the lunch that had become their main meal of the day.

High prices were not what she painted for, but only the high price would gain the acclaim that she did paint for. It was odd that she could feel this touch of disappointment in having reached this plateau, the journey so nearly done. In her life, Alberta thought there had always been more than a touch of sadness in every bit of happiness, a marble swirl cake of plum black and almond white.

A CERTAIN SYMMETRY

Hank, as he watched Owen, thought that he was still the most handsome man he had known, and now that Isaac had come to live with them, Hank saw more of the gene pool that had produced such looks. And, if he had never known Owen, Sims would take that most favored position, handsome for other reasons. He was enthralled with them both. Hank knew that these were the secret thoughts he probably would not share with his two lovers.

Looks were one matter, but the inside beauty award would be taken by Sims. Sims had saved him from so many dangerous corners, seeing the danger before anyone else. Hank knew when he went around town with the two men, for dinners and concerts, heads still turned in admiration. He was not ashamed of his own looks, but on his own, heads seldom turned. Viona said early on that both Owen and Sims had the Black Fire, and that one of them turned it on high when the other one was low, as if they were but one person, conserving energy. You could see the wordy side or the painterly side only at one time. Maybe Viona was right.

Once she said that Owen and Sims were like her grandmother's cuckoo clock, which brought out Hansel and Gretel when the weather was good, and the Witch out when the weather was bad. She could never figure who of them was which.

She was talking to Owen and Sims on the front portal chairs, as Hank was doing his thinking while seated on the half-wall. It was mid-summer, with the light evening sky going on for hours after dinner. The ever-present family of rabbits, newly enlarged in number, were munching away at the far end of the front lawn.

"You're quiet, Hank," Sims said. "Something going on at work?"

"No. Just a bout of thinking."

"Risky business."

"I was wondering about one thing," Hank said. "Do you think we should plan to go to Paris for Alberta's new exhibit next week? Can it really be twenty-five years since the last one?"

"I think we ought to," Owen said. "She and Malvina do not have many more years."

"I can certainly go," Viona said.

"Maybe we should," Sims said. "Too bad that I-I-Igor won't be there to make Hank nervous."

"Sad, isn't it?" Hank said. "I feel guilty now about not just giving in to him. How could it have mattered?"

"It would have been the high-point of his life. He has probably had to settle for Leonid Ulensky, your look-alike, but a very poor second by all counts."

"I'll get us all tickets tomorrow," Owen said.

"And let's go to that restaurant again," Viona said. "Where Igor couldn't keep his hands from wandering. I'll bet it is still there."

"By the way, last week I got a letter from Malvina,"

Owen said. "She wrote that a compound of houses has gone on the market for a reduced price, just up the hill in Menton from her and Alberta. It has a large stone main house, several cottages on terraces of olives, and an expansive view of the sea. She says she cannot understand why French real estate is still such a bargain in the 1970s. Give her a call and it is ours."

"Do you think we should look at it while we are there?" Sims asked.

"You two can paint or write anywhere," Hank said, "but what would I do?"

"France must need lawyers, too."

"I've read that Spanish speakers can learn French more easily than others," Viona said.

Sims, enjoying his role as the one who summed things up, said, "There is something right about leaving before the end of the dance, before the orchestra goes out of tune and the bottles are empty. Our Indian Rope Trick — to climb up the coils and away."

The four of them talked about the subject as the evening got darker, imagining themselves uprooted and trying their lives in Europe. Hank knew he would stay with his lovers, wherever they went. Viona said she would like to take on the French fashion world starting with a small, second shop in the south of France. They all expected that Isaac would probably come along as well, now with his new wife, perhaps looking for property himself. Changes for all of them were in the air.

It had never occurred to Hank to have sex with anybody except his two lovers because there had been no one who could match their combined allure. The three of them were lucky that neither death nor impairment had entered their lives, now more than several decades together. Sims talked about the time when love would fade, as if it was immutable and certain, like the water pulling away from shore for good. Why, Hank thought, could it not go on until the very end? It had so far.

They did not have physical love so often now. It had always been Sims who started their nights together, luring them into Owen's bed with a touch of humor or outright lust. His voice alone could cause a tingle in Hank on those nights, saying what particular things he intended to do. Owen would chime in and before a minute or two the love had begun. It was then that language without words again, the wonderful touch that Hank could not describe the next day, the touch that rippled out like circles on the surface of a pond, bouncing back again from the far side.

There was a place on the back of his neck that Sims knew could open up the worlds of joy. Some nights all of them seemed to be turning themselves over to the same clock, waiting for the hands to reach the highest part of the circle at the same time, as high as they could go together. These were the nights that Hank remembered.

He imagined that he would die first, giving a certain symmetry to their lives, leaving Owen and Sims together at the far end of their run, as they had been before they dropped by the Esso station for gas. What if they so long ago had taken the other, more direct, road into town and not come by his corner? Hank thought he would never have met them, never be going again with them to Paris in a week, never having another carafe of red wine on the street-side tables, never entertaining the thought of moving to France. He might still be filling the tanks of automobiles with gasoline, scraping the windshields of the encrusted brown moths, gnats, and yellow butterflies, and sweeping by hand that final crescent on the glass with a clean, white cloth. How odd, how much a matter of chance it all was.